To Finn

with

F...

[signature] M^c*[...]*

6/9/2³

Tales from the Battlefield

A collection of short stories and poems

Meet the Contributors

Marco Giannasi

Marco is the successful proprietor of the *Battlefield Rest* restaurant. He has a Master of Art from the Istituto Passaglia in Lucca. Marco transformed a dilapidated former tram halt into a very popular Italian eatery which has become a landmark for diners both in the south-side and further afield.

He has also conserved an iconic building in the Battlefield area and, indeed, has made part of it an apiary which produces locally produced honey and helps preserve the local bee population.

He has recently turned his hand to writing short stories with a distinctive culinary theme.

Hugh V. McLachlan

Hugh is an emeritus professor of Applied Philosophy at Glasgow Caledonian University and has published several books on social policy, social philosophy and ethical issues. He is also a renowned authority on the history of witchcraft in Scotland and is a regular speaker on the subject.

He continues to contribute articles for newspapers and online newscasts as well as appearances on television and radio.

Forthcoming novel Call me 'Lucky': Chance and Choice in the Re-creation of Ms James Warren.

Frank Chambers
Frank is a musician and teacher who now concentrates on writing He has published two novels, Lost on Main Street and The Busker of Buenos Aires and also co-wrote the songs on two albums by Kandella, Flying High and Are You Listening.

Alex Meikle
Alex was formerly a CEO of several third sector social care organisations in Glasgow. He also spent many years working in the addiction services in the city and has just recently retired. He still provides a consultancy on social care and community-based issues. Alex's main interest is writing, and he published his first novel, *Deception Road*, which is a political thriller set in Glasgow, in 2017. This is the first of four thrillers centred on the career of MI5 officer, Eddie Macintyre. The second novel in the quartet, *Caledonia Snack*, will be released on Amazon in March 2023.

Henry Buchanan
Henry is a Literary Studies scholar and has published several works, including interpretations of Dostoevsky's *Crime and Punishment* and Shakespeare's *A Midsummer Night's Dream*. He has also published reviews in literary journals. He attended Langside College and read Social Sciences at the Glasgow Caledonia University.

Palma McKeown

Palma McKeown is Scots-Italian and lives in Motherwell. She has been published in various poetry magazines and anthologies. Much of her poetry is inspired by her family and the surreal (often the same thing.) She is a qualified hypnotherapist, an ex-BBC subtitler and spent a few years working in Saffron Walden, Essex, with the job title "World Alcohol Manager." She has long been a fan of vintage and now has three stores on Etsy: Blithe Spirit Vintage, Luckenbooth Vintage and Kingfisher Vintage UK.

Rosalyn Barclay

Rosalyn is a former nurse who has worked in several Glasgow hospitals, including the Western Infirmary and the former Southern General, as well as in health centres across the city. A former Chair of the Langside, Battlefield and Camphill Community Council she has been very engaged in community activities.

She also presents a popular music programme on the CamGlen local radio station and has had many music personalities as guests on her programme.

Ros has published several books based on her nursing experiences as well as her role as a radio presenter.

Jonny Aitken

Jonny grew up in the south side of Glasgow and was educated at Hutchesons Grammar School.

He has been working with film and movie images for most of my life.

Duncan McDonald

Duncan is a retired environmental technician. In a previous life he worked in naval shipyards, maintaining an interest in all things nautical ever since. Strange things happen at sea and Duncan's stories reveal the circumstances behind those occurrences. He hopes soon to be involved in the return of HMS Ambuscade to the Clyde.

Lizzie Allan

Lizzie graduated from Glasgow University with a Master of Arts degree. She gained a P.G.C.E and has recently retired from her profession as a secondary school teacher. She has an SEN qualification and has worked and volunteered in the SEN sector.

Lizzie enjoys writing short stories in various genres and writing poetry – often with a touch of humour.

She also enjoys painting, crafting and playing the ukulele.

Contents

Cocao Bean/The Fork

By Marco Giannasi

We are in the distant 1500s and a machete stroke opens a spectacular view in front of me. Those splendid leaves which had cradled and protected me during my birth from the humid heat and those unforgettable evenings full of sounds and songs of rare birds, have given way to reveal a city of lush, tall evergreen trees called Amazonia with it's ceaseless and chaotic landscape of luxurious jaguars, lazy sloths, funny cabybaras, accompanied by the hidden background songs of toucans and kingfishers.

Each of us is born with different identities, shapes, qualities, tastes, intelligences, whether humans, animals, objects, plants, insects and so on. I discovered myself to be a cocao bean.

So, after the machete stroke opened me to the world, I wondered, where will I go? What will they do with me and all the other beans surrounding me?

At this point of my journey, I found myself inside a pod together with about thirty other beans, which like me, were of a creamy white colour. But, after been startled by the sound of the machete, we were unceremoniously ejected from the pod down to Earth like being stranded in an elevator hurtling to the ground and landing with an impact that even Newton would have noticed.

Having come to ground in such abrupt circumstances, I felt in bad shape and with such a dishevelled appearance that I could have emerged from a scrap yard. Since I was a grain

1

and not baptized with any name, I thought of calling myself Rococo. Don't ask me why but I considered that it had a distinctly mischievous and exuberant cheek about it. I was surrounded by two different varieties of grains: one was similar to myself with a porcelain type appearance. I surmised we were all from the same Criollo family. The other variety, however, which were uglier and rougher than us, were probably from the Forastero family. Despite the latter's imperfections, I considered both families of grains were certainly quite valuable.

The day was hot and humid with an unstable and unpredictable air as if a storm was about to break. Suddenly, we heard explosions, flames, sparks and a smoke so black, accompanied by a very unpleasant smell, that it made me certain that a catastrophe was imminent. Then, as suddenly as it began, everything calmed down and I realized that it was only caused by the engine of our infamous van which started moving. To my surprise, I noticed that the driver was our caretaker, Paco.

The journey proceeded along a very rough and bumpy road, and we seemed to hit every pothole along it, causing us to jostle and collide against each, leading to tensions between us.

When we finally arrived at our destination, we were placed on a table. At this point, our so-called guardian, Paco, very delicately picked us from the pod we were in and enclosed us in a delicious and sweet pulp which transformed us into cocao beans. But I wasn't sure what they wanted to do with us.

From here they took us to ferment, placing us in buckets which were covered with banana leaves. After this, we were left for a few days. During this time, I grew more concerned about what would happen to all of us?

We were all close to each other in the dark without light or air and with a smell that every day became more offensive. Finally, after days of enduring this ordeal, we were taken outside into the sun to dry.

Paco at this point, reappeared, raking us vigorously back and forth inducing in us a sensation of madness and freedom with a pleasant tickle that pervaded us. Oh, I can hardly convey to you, the pleasure I felt in absorbing that warm sun; I even caught a tan for the first time, and I must admit, lost a little of the excess weight I had been carrying.

Then, suddenly, while we were all lying, sweetly dreaming, basking quietly in the sun without any worries, Paco reappeared and began to select only the best beans. Unfortunately, I too was chosen. He collected us in tubs and put us in the oven to make us toast. O my God, is this the end for us? I prayed I would not be burned, until I passed out, losing all sense of what was happening.

When I awakened, everything was silent around me. I was afraid to fully wake up as I had no sense nor strength to move. I had completely lost any sensation of my normal shape or form! Was this the end for me?

When I finally did become fully aware of my surroundings, I was astonished to be aware that, yes, I definitely still existed, but my shape had turned into a sweet creamy substance of a scent so sweet and delicious that, to be honest, even I was becoming aroused and excited by the idea of what I could create and what taste I would be.

.   .   .   .

The Fork

I was born in the 1930s from pure silver worked to perfection by a high-quality craftsman who went by the nickname of the "Fusino". He was so scrupulous that it took him half-a-day to make me, because the last detail on the royal seal was not "perfect". I mention the royal seal to give you an idea of the class my "look" today still belongs to. I am slender, elegant, shiny and when you clasp me in your hand, you also feel a little sensual with my beautiful shape that lets itself be warmed by your fingers. I am telling you my story since I was first placed in a drawer encased in ruby red velvet along with many colleagues of mine, all lying side-by-side waiting to begin our duty.

As a high-class fork, of quality, distinction and lightness, I started my career at the Grand Palace hotel on the shore of Lake Lugano in Switzerland. The first night was quiet and very tense because we would be serving dinner to the royal family of the United Kingdom.

Seven o' clock and, suddenly, you hear an almost seismic vibration which makes all the glassware tremble, including the drawer where we'd been placed in. It is "Bernardo" the waiter, wearied and bored by too many years of repetitive duties arid rigorously enforced orders. He approaches us with a heavy step.

With clammy and tired shaky hands, he picks us up one-at-a-time with great kindness, concern and respect (again an indication of the professionalism, pride and serious approach he took to his job. Then, as if it were a ceremony, he would place us, now polished and smooth, on an intricately embroidered white virgin tablecloth.

4

Suddenly, I find myself facing the ceiling next to an old fork of the first course. Being so shiny and new, I appeared in such contrast to the other cutlery. I could not hide my excitement and pride to be at this historic event, but at the same time embarrassed to stand out more than those next to me. I realized that my colleagues had been set at another table by chance and I had been placed among an older, but still fashionable set. By now they had fed many characters and dignities, some vulgar and disgusting while at other times they had entered the most pleasant and polite mouths which exhibited the most artistic expressions of pleasure, symbolic of a sense of great satisfaction with the taste and quality of the lunch just served.

However, since I was the final fork, the one intended for dessert, I would have to wait until all the previous courses had been served and eaten, for me to shine and be the last star of this great evening.

At this point I was wondering to whom I would serve that exquisite millefeuille cake made of a delicious and fragile pastry that delicately enclosed a soft and fluffy cream soaked in drops of maraschino liqueur to excite the palate, just waiting for those guests still carried away by their greed. The air was full of the noises and sounds of glasses, cutlery and plates mixed with laughter, voices and wild sounds.

Then suddenly, as after a great storm a quiet penetrates the hall. Stomachs sag with exhaustion but still trying to find a space to consume the last spoonful of that gorgeous dessert!

As, during a mass, believers gather in a moment of silence, so the guests at the moment of entrance to the Dolce, gather in bizarre shapes due to too much eating and drinking like flocks of animals waiting for their prey with fixed expressions, but still greedy for more.

The first portion is prepared with great care, particular attention being paid to the dripping of the hot chocolate complete with a gilt leaf that adorns like a decoration the last final touch before serving. I feel like the prima ballerina of La Scala who enters the stage for her first public show. Like her I wait for a warm applause which vanishes in an instant as reality strikes as I see for the first time who I'm about to face with my portion of Millefoglie; a very unpleasant guest with badly educated teeth and nightmarish caries and a tinned and turbulent breath. Thank goodness, being such a rough person, he ate the dessert rapidly so that I was in and out of that hideous cave of a mouth very quickly as he finished the dessert in a short time. Thanks to the waiter on duty, I was quickly freed from that horror to go to the kitchen and be washed and dried.

Poor me! Desperate to get rid of that bad taste left by that vulgar mouth, I am plunged with all the others in a hot and perfumed foam bath enveloped in bubbles like little wings of angels as if to reassure us that we were now safe and secure from all those big threatening faces!

After being dried and polished I was tired and a little bewildered before being placed back with all the other forks and falling asleep.

It was about three in the morning when I was suddenly awakened by a noise very close to me. A girl's small hand picked me up very gently and with great care placed me in her apron. What was happening I asked myself? Why is it just me that's being selected from the rest of the cutlery? Where am I being taken to? I don't want to leave my colleagues and I'm afraid I'll never see them again! Hours passed without a sound except for a gentle noise that was perhaps a child snoring. Then an alarm went off and a voice calls everyone to breakfast. To breakfast! Where am I?

Then it dawned on me what had happened. I had been stolen by the young daughter of the dishwasher who had taken me from the kitchen to their home.

Looking at the cutlery and plates on the table I could see that this family was very poor. How am I going to get back to my dear friends?

Abruptly, the father of the house picked me up and said in authoritative tones to his wife: "But this fork is made of pure silver! By goodness, we can melt it down and sell it and make some money!"

Oh my God, help me, I don't need this! But what can I do?

HOW TO BE SCOTS-ITALIAN

By Palma McKeown

Get a head start by having a first name
that doesn't really go with your second name.
Your parents were just trying to keep everyone happy.
Keep a bottle of Lacryma Christi for when
your Auntie Anna calls in unexpectedly.
Hide the jar of instant coffee in case
she comes into the kitchen and dust off
the old metal coffee pot that unscrews in the middle.
Put out that panettone you got at Christmas
then watch as she scoffs all the Tunnock's Teacakes.
Learn to sidle down side streets or
melt into shop doorways when you see
old Mr D'Ambrosio coming because, despite
the fact he's lived here for over sixty years,
you still can't make out a word he's saying.
Be prepared to serve sausage rolls and salami di Milano
at Hogmanay parties and give equal play time
to Jimmy Shand and Dean Martin.
You're just trying to keep everyone happy.
Listen politely to your Auntie Carmen from Coatbridge
when she phones at three in the morning to ask
if everything's ok because she's had a dream
about you and the number 62
which signifies death and pestilence.
Try unsuccessfully to get back to sleep.

Feel torn when Italy is playing Scotland at football
until the crowd starts to sing 'Flower of Scotland'
and a wee tear runs down your cheek.
Try not to get bitter that you never knew
your Italian granddad because during the war
he was taken away by two Scottish policemen
in the middle of the night, herded onto a ship
and was lost at sea when it was torpedoed.
Churchill was just trying to keep everyone happy.

[First published in Talking About Lobsters, New Writing
Scotland 34, ASLS]

Twitter: @palma_mc

THE SPECTRE

By Alex Meikle

It was ironic that the "spectre", as he called it, happened as Dougie Conroy was reading Gilbert Matheson's *Science and Rationality*. He'd just dozed off from the ponderous text and was in that lovely narcotic twilight place before sleep, when a slight movement of the bedroom curtains, caused by a breeze from the open windows on this mild February night, made him open his eyes.

He became fully awake. At the foot of his bed stood a tall man wearing an olive-green raincoat. He had bright, piercing eyes which stared straight at, if not through him. Silvery grey streaks ran through his receding brown hair. He stood there against the backdrop of the bay window in the small bedroom.

Baffled and bewildered as to how he hadn't heard the guy come into the room, Dougie fleetingly closed his eyes. Puzzlement gave way to fear about the guy's intentions as he looked again at the foot of the bed. The guy had vanished. Dougie rose, shook his head, and looked again. There was just the bay window, the dark-brown curtains and another slight breeze rippling gently through them. The room was empty.

Dougie stood up and looked at the bedroom door. It was closed and he hadn't heard any movement. Now fully awake and still quite fearful, he opened the door. The corridor leading to a right-angled turn at the head of the staircase was deserted. He had two flat mates: Pete and Steve. Pete's bedroom adjoined his. He knew that both Pete and Steve, whose bedroom was at the top of the landing, were out. Steve at a club and Pete with his girlfriend for the night.

He knocked on Pete's door in case he'd come back unheard. 'Pete, you in?' Silence. He slowly opened the door. The room was deserted. He closed the door and walked up to Steve's room, calling out and opening the door. It was also empty.

He looked down the staircase. Nothing. Descending the staircase, he tried the front door, the sheen of the streetlamps refracted through the frosted pane of glass on the door. It was locked, as indeed it should have been, as he'd locked it himself a few hours ago.

There was a living room with an adjacent dining space and a kitchen at the back on the ground floor. All were empty, silent, and undisturbed. The back door was also secure. 'What the hell just happened?' he thought to himself. He switched the lights on downstairs and made a cup of tea in the kitchen, his hands slightly shaking.

As he waited on the kettle boiling, Dougie reflected that he was a rational man, who didn't believe in ghosts, certainly not in "apparitions" of middle-aged men lurking at the bottom of your bed! Absurd. And yet there'd been something tangible, substantial even, about the figure he'd seen. Not some floating, wraith like phantom.

But it couldn't be. The house was empty and locked. It would be impossible for the "man" to have entered or left without, at the least, causing a racket. No, he'd been half-asleep and what he'd "seen" was probably the dying embers of a very lucid dream which he'd read about in the psychology section on his previous undergraduate course at Glasgow University.

Having drunk his tea and fortified himself the "spectre" was a dream, Dougie went back to bed. But he didn't fall asleep immediately, as he still felt slightly disturbed. He tuned his bedside radio onto the BBC World Service and read a Michael Moorcock sci-fi novel until he drifted off to sleep. He was vaguely aware, at some point, of Steve coming back from his club, no doubt accompanied by a young lady, before resuming his sleep.

Dougie Conroy, as noted, regarded himself very much as a man of science and rationality as that tedious book he'd been reading was titled. The book was recommended reading on the Philosophy of Science course, an option which Dougie had decided to take to accompany his Management Sciences postgraduate degree at Camden & Islington Polytechnic in North London.

Management Sciences was a world away from the radical and challenging syllabus that was Social Sciences at Glasgow University in the late '70s and early '80s. Coming from a strong Catholic background, Dougie had been confronted with an array of exciting new ideas and concepts which revolutionized his ways of thinking. In contrast, Management Science was quite dull and pragmatic. Moreover, the idea of being a manager, of bossing people, even exploiting them, sat uneasily with his left-wing principles.

But, since graduating, he'd been unemployed and signing on the dole. Lack of money coupled with heavy pressure from his parents to get a job, compelled him to search for post-graduate courses with better "employability" prospects in an era of mass unemployment. Social Science degrees, for the most part, were not good passports to the world of work epitomized by the witticism: Question: 'What do you say to a social science student after they've graduated?' Answer: 'Two cheeseburgers and a Coke, please.'

Back in March the previous year, with tensions increasingly fraught in the Conroy household over Dougie's jobless status, he'd come across a glossy advert in the *Guardian's* Education supplement promoting the Management Sciences postgraduate course at Camden & Islington Poly. It ticked a lot of boxes: He'd be out the house. He should have better employment prospects after the course. And he'd be in London. He applied, went down for an exam and interview, passed, and was accepted; the course was commencing in October.

Despite it being the first he'd spent any length of time away from home, Dougie settled in well. Students, worldwide, are all in the same boat. High spirited but penniless and occasionally bailed out by parents. Living on meagre grants and loans, but still managing to have a lively social life. The group Dougie was accommodated with in a drab Edwardian four storey communal flat off the Holloway Road, were no exception. A mixed bunch of undergraduates with only one other postgraduate, Brad, like Dougie a guy in his twenties from Liverpool who he shared a room and got on well with as, indeed, he did with all of them.

Boys lived in the first two floors of the "house", girls on the remaining two floors. Within days they were mixing well, the effective "common room" being the kitchen on the ground floor where everyone gathered. Very quickly in those first few days, Dougie took a shine to a girl with fair skin, freckled face, and wispy light blond hair. He also loved her lilting, west country burr. Marilyn was from rural Gloucestershire amidst the Cotswold Hills. Dougie was as intrigued by her as he was attracted to her. She was equally

13

intrigued by him, drawn to his strong Glasgow accent and flirtatiously shocked by his socialist views. He, in turn, was astounded by her robust support for the Tory government.

Back in Glasgow, everyone Dougie knew was a socialist of some description. Fellow students, friends, family, neighbours, virtually all around him were on the left and abominated the Tories, particularly the Prime Minister, Margaret Thatcher. He was astonished, on arrival in London, to find so many people supportive of the government. Sure, there were plenty of left "activists" on campus, but most of his fellow students were either politically indifferent or tended to the right. And this amid mass unemployment, rampant poverty, and an increasingly bitter and divisive miner's strike. Dougie was perplexed.

He didn't hold back his views with Marilyn, nor she with him and the sparks created seemed to make their attraction stronger. Come the following June, and the end of the exams (she was studying chemistry), she'd invited him to spend a weekend with her parents, sister, and brother. Now that, he thought, was going to be an *interesting* weekend.

Despite his initial apprehension, he buckled down and quite enjoyed some of the syllabus, particularly Marketing which, in Dougie's estimation, was basically applying psychology on how to get people to part with their money.

He also enjoyed the Philosophy of Science course which confirmed both his certainty about the primacy of science and his belief that religion, spirituality, mysticism, the occult, was all superstitious tosh, "opium of the people" in Karl Marx's brilliant phrase. For that reason, he'd looked forward to reading Mathieson's tome but was disappointed by how dull and repetitive it was. Still, it didn't detract from his belief that the material world was all there was.

By the turn of the year, he'd settled in well and his relationship with Marilyn was blossoming. The only dark spot was his roommate, Brad, leaving to move in with his girlfriend. His replacement, Clive, was frankly annoying, despite, ironically, being a Labour Party supporter. He also had BO. Within ten days, he could no longer stand sharing the same room with him.

As the house rules forbade him to move in with Marilyn (which she shared with another girl anyway), Dougie was compelled to find another flat. Fortunately, another male student in the house had a friend whose own flat in Haringey had a room going vacant following the departure of one of the residents. The friend was Pete and Dougie, and Marilyn went to view it.

The "flat" was in fact a two-storey house set amidst a row of houses a couple of hundred yards back from Haringey's main drag, Green Lanes. It was a typical blokes' house. Tidy, but austere and functional. Certainly. a contrast to the chaotic friendliness and colour of the Holloway house. Dougie was reluctant, but Marilyn talked him into it. In truth, there was no privacy in Holloway, which did grate with him. There was the odious figure of Clive. Above all, and what clinched it, they would have a room where Marilyn could spend the night with him on a regular basis. Whereas, back at Holloway, with its shared rooms, they had to be more furtive.

Dougie moved into the first-floor front room of the house in late January. It was a lot quieter and spartan than his previous digs. Pete and Steve were peaceful and studious flatmates. Steve did bring a lot of girls back, but he took them immediately to his room and didn't disturb Dougie. Marilyn spent lots of lovely nights with him and he got far more studying done. He'd inquired of his flat mates why the previous resident in his room had left. Both appeared genuinely perplexed at this, saying only that he'd been a quiet guy who'd kept himself to himself and one day announced he was leaving, packed his stuff and was gone. No explanation given. After the "spectre", Dougie wondered if this had any bearing on his predecessor's hasty departure. But he dismissed this. Surely, the guy would have said something.

The "spectre" had happened months ago. Nothing had occurred since and he had never spoken of it, not least to Pete or Steve, nor Marilyn. Life proceeded normally. As Winter gave way to Spring and the dreaded exam season loomed, Dougie became immersed in his studies as did Marilyn which meant she stayed over less during this time. The flat mates also spent more time in their rooms and in the evenings when they were cooking meals in the kitchen, Dougie saw far more of them and got to know them better. By the time the exams came around in May, he'd put the "spectre" to the back of his mind and dismissed it as an illusion. All was well in a material world.

One Thursday evening all three were in the house at the same time. Dougie and Steve were in the kitchen cooking, respectively, fish fingers with processed peas, and a Vesta chow mein. Pete, who was in the living room listening to music on the radio, had already eaten. Dougie brought his dinner into the living room while Steve was finishing simmering his. From the kitchen doorway, Steve asked:

'Chaps, what's your exams tomorrow?'

Pete answered first. 'Haven't got any. Next one's Tuesday.'

'I've got a day of freedom too,' Dougie put in, 'but I'll probably spend most of it studying.'

'Great,' said Steve, still standing at the kitchen entrance. 'I've got none either. Tell you want, why don't we pool money together and get some booze from the offy? Some cans or wine or whatever.'

'Love to, but I've got studying,' Dougie replied. 'Still got three exams to go.'

'I'm the same,' Pete added. 'In the middle of it right now.'

'Oh, come on boys,' Steve protested. 'One night off won't do any harm. We can have a long sleep-in and pick up the studying in the afternoon or evening. I don't know about you lads, but I need a break. And this is a first,' he went on, pointing at Dougie, 'a bloody Scotsman knocking back the prospect of booze. That's a new one on me!'

Pete and Dougie looked at each other, Dougie's half-finished plate of fish fingers and peas on his lap. Pete broke first.

'I suppose I could do one night.' Dougie swithered longer. Eventually, aware of the focused stares of the other two on him, he relented.

'Oh, all right. I suppose a night off will be ok.'

'Brilliant!' Steve said. 'We'll check how much we have and get some drinks in, have a relaxing night.'

After dinner, they searched jackets and coats in their rooms and uncovered enough spare cash for a decent sized "cargo" of booze – twelve cans of lager and three bottles of relatively cheap wine – which they purchased at the nearest off-sales. They had enough change between them to also buy crisps and chocolate bars. On the way back Steve revealed he had some dope, enough for a few joints. After hearing that, Dougie thought there was little chance of him studying the next day.

They got stuck into the booze and had demolished two bottles of the wine and half the cans by midnight, getting high and unwinding from the stresses of constant exams and studying. Steve rolled and lit a joint which he passed to the others. Dougie had smoked dope many times but there was a fair strength to this hash, and he felt comfortably blasted after inhaling a big draw.

Inevitably, they started giggling and talking loudly as they got stoned. At some point Pete remarked:

'This is great. We couldn't really do this when the other guy was living in your room, Dougie.'

'Remind me again, what he was like?' Dougie asked.

'A weirdo', Steve said bluntly. 'Never spoke a word, never learnt a thing about him, stayed in his room a lot or went out, but there were never any friends, even family or girls. Nothing.'

'What was he studying?'

'Couldn't even tell you,' Pete answered.

'And then,' Steve continued, 'one day, at the start of January, he's suddenly off. Just packed up and left.'

'Why?' Dougie asked again.

'Dunno', Steve replied, shaking his head.

'That *is* just weird!' Dougie agreed. He went on. 'Do you know where he moved to?'

'Not a dickie. Just vanished.'

'Did he owe any rent?'

'No, he was sound there. I spoke to the landlord. He was up to date with the rent. He even got his deposit back!'

'Lucky bastard! Hope we get ours back,' Dougie said ruefully.

There was a brief silence while Pete opened another can of lager and Steve finished the joint.

'Actually,' Pete said slowly after taking a swallow from his can, 'I had a chat with him just before he left.'

'You never told me that,' Steve said sharply. 'When was this?'

'It was the morning he left. You were still in bed. I think you'd come in about three with someone. I didn't want to, ah, wake you.'

'Yeah, ok, got you,' Steve conceded. 'But you could have told me later.'

'You vanished for two weeks after that!' I thought you'd done a runner!'

Steve virtually cringed and admitted, shaking his head: 'That's right, sorry. It was that crazy girl. Thought I was truly in love that time. Lucky escape.'

'And by the time you came back,' Pete went on, 'he'd long gone and then I got word Dougie was looking for a room and it seemed like history.'

'Yeah, true,' Steve agreed. 'So, anyway, what did Mr. Personality have to say to you before he upped sticks?'

Pete looked away and avoided eye contact before bursting into a short laugh.

'Come on, fess up, what was it?' Steve urged him.

Pete shook his head. 'It was strange, really weird.' He took another sip of his lager, before resuming.

'It was a Saturday morning. He knocked on my door, looking, what would you say, flushed and agitated. There was a wild look in his eyes.'

'He always looked a bit out of sorts,' Steve put in. 'Had he been drinking or had a smoke?'

'No, I don't think so. Least, I didn't smell anything off him. No, this was something else. He was genuinely scared.'

'Scared?' Steve and Dougie responded, almost in unison.

'Yeah,' Pete nodded, his eyes wide open. 'He was rattled. Look, shut up and just let me tell it because I've not spoken about it to anyone before.'

Steve poured himself another glass of wine while Dougie clutched hold of his can, thinking he knew where this might be going. Pete carried on.

'I let him into my room, and he said he was leaving, now, right away. I asked him why, of course. He didn't say at first, so I asked him if it was anything to do with us,' Pete looked at Steve. 'But he shook his head, saying firmly "no". He just stood there, and I couldn't think of anything else to say and I wished him well and was about to ask him where he was going when he blurted out that his room was "haunted" and there was a ghost in it.'

'What?' Steve almost shouted. Dougie remained silent but was completely alert now, despite the dope and the alcohol.

'Yep. He said he saw a ghost. A big guy with scary eyes at his bedside.'

Rolling another joint, Steve said, dismissively, 'Been at the wacky all night, eh?'

Pete disagreed. 'No way. He might have been strange, but I don't think he even smoked fags. Besides, I never smelt anything from his room, and, by God, you can smell this all right.' He referred to the acrid aroma that now pervaded the living room.

'So,' Pete resumed, 'he said it wasn't the first-time strange things had happened in the room like things going missing and weird noises when the house was empty and so on. He was really rattled. Said he'd had "enough" and then just strode out. I was flabbergasted. Didn't know what to say. Anyway, he was gone soon afterwards. I reckon he was ill, up here,' Pete pointed to his head, 'poor sod. Besides,' he said, looking at Dougie, 'you've been here, what, four months. Nothing strange has happened to you in that room, eh?'

For a few moments Dougie kept his silence, staring intently at his can. Then, he said, haltingly:

'Well, I don't know how to say this, chaps, but eh,' he coughed, 'you see. Aw hell. You see I saw something too in that room.'

'What?' Steve asked, the two of them looking straight at him.

'Just like the guy before me, I saw a big guy at the foot of my bed with piercing eyes. It felt they were going right through me. Just a second, mind, and it was gone. It was back in February. You two were out and, no, I hadn't been at the booze or any dope. I was stone cold sober. It really spooked me!'

Steve had his hands out wide. 'Why didn't you tell us?'

'Come on, would you have believed me? Besides, nothing else has ever happened, unlike with my predecessor. Nothing. And, up until right now, I'd dismissed it. Not even spoken to Marilyn about it. And,' he gave a brief laugh, 'if I did, it'd be the last time I'd ever get her into that bedroom!'

'Too true,' Steve agreed.

'This is really spooky,' Pete remarked. 'One guy, yeah you could argue it's something to do just with him. Like I say, maybe mental health problems. But two separate guys experiencing the same thing? And you're normal, unlike him!'

'Thanks,' Dougie responded.

'It *is* pretty strange,' Steve remarked, finishing rolling the joint and lighting it.

It was past one, and a silence descended on the room. In truth, all three of them were feeling unsettled, Dougie foremost, as all the troubling, uncanny thoughts he'd had that February night when he saw the "spectre", came back with a vengeance.

Passing the joint onto Pete, Steve said: 'tell you what, why don't we test if this house is haunted.'

'How?' Pete asked.

'Simple. If it's here, we'll communicate with it by using a Ouija board.'

'No way, man. You don't know what you could start with that,' Pete said as he drew on the joint. 'You could open up a bloody portal to the other side, or whatever you call it.'

'Oh, come on, Pete,' Steve replied. 'You make it sound like something out of *Poltergeist* for Christ's sake! We'll just ask if there's something there. We won't go any further than that. I've done it before, trust me.'

'Where have you done it before?' Dougie asked, as Pete passed the joint to him.

'Back home, in Blackburn. It was my aunt's house and we communicated with an old lady who'd died decades earlier and used to live there. It was spooky, all right, but quite good. My aunt was a bit of a psychic and said that if you communicate with a trapped spirit then you can help to make it less restless and troublesome, and you can guide spirits onto the next stage in the afterlife or whatever.'

'Aw, look,' Dougie came in, waving the joint about him, 'I don't believe in this, ok? But I know I saw something and that guy before did too. I can't explain this. But,' he shook his head, 'I'm a bit stoned...'

'...Yeah, this hash is good, all right,' Steve butted in.

'...and I'm half-cut, so, I'll probably regret this, but let's do this, even just for a laugh. Tell me, how you gonna do it? There's no Ouija board in the house as far as I'm aware.'

'You don't need a real board. Bits of paper will do. Leave it to me.' Steve left the room.

'This is mad, no, worse than mad, it's dangerous,' Pete said worriedly, can in hand.

Dougie shrugged his shoulders. 'Don't take it too seriously, Pete.'

'Yeah, but you did see something in your room, right?'

Dougie nodded.

'Then I hope he knows what he's doing.'

Steve returned with an A4 notepad which he tore a single sheet from. He then proceeded methodically to tear the sheet into small circular strips, twenty-six of which he labelled A to Z with a black ink pen. A further ten he labelled 0 to 9. With Pete's reluctant assistance, he brought the large circular, teak dining table at the corner of the room (which, to Dougie's knowledge, none of them had ever actually dined at) into the middle of the room moving aside two chairs and the settee. He brought three of the four dining chairs over and bade Pete and Dougie to sit at the table.

'You've definitely done this before,' Dougie remarked.

'No, I've just watched my auntie closely,' he replied.

With the three of them sitting at the table, Steve tore another strip of A4 and tore that further in half. One half of the paper he placed in the middle of the table and drew a five-angled pentagram on it also in black ink. Beside the paper pentangle, he placed two more strips of paper to the left and right. On the left-hand strip he wrote "Yes" and on the right "No". The circular pieces of paper bearing the letters of the alphabet he placed in a wide circle around the pentangle in a clockwise direction with "A" at midnight. He then put the numbered pieces in an inner circle around the pentangle with "0" at the top. Finally, from the kitchen he produced some seller tape and a small glass. He tore the tape into strips and secured the paper letters, numbers, and pentangle to the dining table. Moving the glass, which served as an improvised planchette over the "Ouija Board", he satisfied himself it was tightly bound in place and wouldn't be disturbed by the moving glass.

Steve sat at the table and stretched out his arms. 'Ok chaps, ready?' He placed his finger on the rim of the glass which was the cue for the others to do so as well.

'Oops! Forgot something.'

He rose and went back to the kitchen. They could hear him rummaging around before coming back with a candle secured in a holder on a saucer. He lit the candle and placed it on the mantlepiece before switching the light off. They were bathed in a glow of flickering light from the candle, the room curtains having been drawn earlier.

'Mustn't forget, candlelight only to allow the spirits freedom to move,' Steve said, resuming his seat at the table.

'This is so wrong,' Pete said shaking his head, the others ignored him.

With their three forefingers on the glass, Steve intoned: 'Is there anyone there?'

Nothing, only the spectral light from the candle. Steve asked again: 'Is there anyone there?' Still nothing. Dougie felt a weird sensation go through him which the rationalist in him attributed to the ambience of the room. Steve looked entranced and focused on the Board while Pete appeared apprehensive.

Steve asked a third time if anyone was there. After a few seconds, this time the glass appeared to move, slowly at first but gently picking up momentum. Dougie felt the glass move but didn't feel he was applying pressure to it. He looked at the other two. Steve had his eyes closed, entranced. Pete looked terrified. 'I'm not moving it,' he whispered.

'Shush,' Steve instructed.

The glass made its' way across the Board to the "Yes" piece of paper and stopped.

"Who are you?' Steve asked. The glass didn't move. Steve asked a few more times to no avail. Then he changed tack, asking:

'If you are there, please let us know who you are? Please spell out for us who you are?'

The glass started to move once more. Again, Dougie didn't feel he was applying any pressure on it. Making its' way seemingly inexorably to the outer circle with the letters, the glass stopped at the letter "C". It stayed there for a few seconds before moving across the circle to "O", then onto "S", followed by "T" and moving quite rapidly onto the top of the circle pausing at "A" before, finally, shifting, again quite fast, onto the inner numbers circle and stopping at "9" where it stayed.

Steve moved his finger from the glass, prompting the others to do so too. He wrote on his A4 pad which he had on his lap and looked around at them.

'COSTA 9. That mean anything to you?'

Dougie and Pete both shook their heads firmly, Pete saying: 'nowt'.

'Ok', Steve said, 'but we're getting somewhere. Let's continue.' He put his fingers back on the rim of the glass followed by the other two.

'How long have you been here?' Steve asked. The glass didn't move. For the next three minutes, which seemed an eternity in that atmosphere, Steve, with increasing desperation, asked how long whatever it was had lived there, but the glass remained firmly stuck at "9". Dougie was about to say to Steve, 'this is pointless', when the glass suddenly started moving again, even more rapidly than before, the three of them struggling to keep their fingers on it as it traced the following letters:

"I" "H" "A" "T" "E". Dougie and Pete didn't need Steve to write that one up for them. All three took their fingers off the glass.

'Oh fuck!' Pete almost shouted. 'This isn't funny,' Dougie said, nervousness and tension enveloping him. Even Steve looked shocked.

'Well, I wasn't expecting that!'.

'That's it.' Pete declared. 'I warned you. Let's finish this NOW!'

'Yes, good call, Pete' Dougie agreed.

'No, no,' Steve said, shaking his head. 'I've seen this before. I get it, its frightening. But it doesn't mean us. It always refers to something in the past of the spirit, most probably at the point when it died. What we can do here is almost like an exorcism gents, and we can move the spirit on to another plane or even just make it settled to get it off its chest, as it were, by naming the person it hates and most likely caused it to die. Its' like a stone tape trapped in here and we, tonight, are the key to unlock it and let it go.'

'You do talk a fair amount of crap,' Dougie scolded him.

'All right,' Steve put his hand up to Dougie, 'just humour me, just let me ask it who it hates, and it'll spell out some meaningless name or mumbo jumbo and we'll let it go.' Steve smiled. 'I'll even roll another joint. I think I've got enough for a last one. Come on!'

Dougie and Pete looked at each other. Both had exasperation mingled with fear on their faces.

'All right,' Dougie spoke for them. 'One last question, who it "hates" and then it's over. Agreed?'

'Absolutely,' Steve concurred. They put their fingers back on the rim of the glass.

'Who do you hate?' Nothing. The question was asked a few more times, but with no response. Then, again suddenly, with surprising speed, the glass moved up to the letter "D" then "O". Dougie removed his finger. The glass stopped instantly. The others also removed their fingers.

'No fucking way! Absolutely no way am I continuing this!' Dougie rose quickly, causing his seat to fall back. He was trembling and a cold sweat was coursing through him. 'Pete, get that light on please!".

Agreeing, Pete rose, saying accusingly at Steve: 'You've gone too far. Definitely,' and switched the light on.

Steve had a milky pallor on his face, which reflected that on the other's faces. He looked shocked and genuinely contrite.

'I'm sorry. That's never happened before. Oh God!'

Pete, who'd remained on his feet said: 'I'm out of here. God alone knows what we've summoned here. I'm going,' and went out the room looking utterly petrified.

They'd all instantly sobered, the hilarity of earlier extinguished by the disturbing turn of events. 'Look, just get that stuff away please, Steve,' Dougie pointed to the Ouija Board on the dining table, the glass still settled ominously on the letter "O.".

'Sure,' Steve replied in a low voice and began tearing the tape off the improvised "board." From the hallway, Dougie could hear the muffled voice of Pete on the telephone. When he'd finished, Pete came into the room.

'I'm going to my girlfriends,' he declared. 'I've told her we've got a gas leak here. See you later, or maybe not.' He left the room.

'I'll take a leaf out of Pete's book,' Dougie said. 'There's no way I'm staying here tonight.' He phoned the Holloway flat. It was well past two and he knew he'd get an earful for disturbing the peace at this hour. One of the guys in the flats answered. Dougie apologized for the late hour and explained it was an "emergency" and he needed to speak to Marilyn. The guy was decent about it and went to knock on her door. After an age, a sleepy Marilyn came on the phone. He told her about the "gas leak," and asked if it was ok if he came over to hers'. She became alert and awake instantly. Her roommate, Julia, was away staying overnight with her boyfriend, so there was no problem coming over.

Dougie packed his things and bade good night to Pete who was waiting for a taxi to get to Peckham where his girlfriend lived. In the living room, Dougie encountered Steve sitting on the settee. He'd rolled himself a last joint. All evidence of the Ouija Board had been cleared and the dining table was back in its corner.

'What you doing tonight? You're not staying here?'

'No. I phoned my pal. He's got a pad just off Upper Street, so I'll head up there when I finish this.'

'Ok, I'm off. Take care. I don't know when I'll be back.'

'I'm really sorry, Dougie. I didn't expect that. I've really upset Pete.'

'We're all rattled. Give it a few days to calm. See you soon.'

He left the house as the taxi was arriving for Pete. Not having enough money himself for a taxi, he walked the thirty minutes it took to Holloway and the warm embrace of Marilyn.

*

That had been five weeks ago. Dougie had stayed three nights with Marilyn in the absence of Julia. He'd returned at the start of the following week. Steve had only spent one night away while Pete was away for five. The reality was that none of them had anywhere else to go.

It took a while for Dougie to acclimatise to the house and his bedroom. He kept the light and radio on at night and read himself to sleep. Dougie never spoke of the strange, disturbing night with either of his flatmates, nor with anyone else. As the exam season progressed, he saw less and less of them as he was ensconced in the library, studying in his room, sitting exams or with Marilyn.

Come mid-June and the end of term, Dougie thought he'd done reasonably well with his exams (he'd get the results in the next few days) and spent the previous weekend with Marilyn's family in the verdant setting of the Cotswalds. It had been a lovely weekend with beautiful, sunny weather. He got on very well with the family, including the father. Yes, they were Tories, but not ogres. He toned down his radicalism. The weekend boded well for his future relationship with Marilyn.

Upon returning to London and the house, he found a note from Steve. He was away for the weekend but would be back on Wednesday to meet with the landlord and get his deposit back. After that, he was moving back to Blackburn; he'd got a trainee position in his father's tailor's shop. Steve also wrote that Pete had moved in permanently with his girlfriend to a new flat but would also be at the Wednesday meeting. Dougie put the note down, thinking he couldn't really picture Steve selling suits for a living.

The phone rang. It was his mum to tell him that she'd been frantically trying to get him over the weekend. His Uncle Andy had died suddenly from a suspected heart attack and the funeral was the following Wednesday in Glasgow. He apologized for not being around but assured her he would come back home for the funeral. Putting the phone down, he felt a genuine pang of affection and sorrow for his Uncle Andy, who from childhood had been one of his favourites. He left a note for Steve and Pete that he wouldn't make the Wednesday meeting because of a family bereavement, and he would arrange to meet with the landlord separately.

He never saw them again and travelled by bus up to Glasgow for the funeral. Before leaving, he arranged with the landlord to meet on the Monday the week after to get his deposit.

He stayed in Glasgow for over a week. When he arrived back in London on the Friday, Marilyn informed him by phone that she was viewing a flat in Camden that evening. Would he like to view it with her? Indeed, would he consider sharing with her? He didn't have to give much thought to that. He'd missed her terribly since coming back from Gloucestershire and resolved that he did want to live with her. Yes, he thought, 'I'm in love.'

The other big development came by post. A letter informed him that he'd been accepted for a trainee management position with a large telecom company in the City of London, conditional on passing his exams. He'd been encouraged to apply by one of his course tutors back in May. The interview had gone well, but he'd heard nothing since. Assuming he would pass the exams, this was great news. He'd be earning in London and could help to support Marilyn who still had another two years of her course to go.

She, of course was delighted at Dougie's news when they met up that afternoon. They viewed the flat in Camden that evening. It was grubby and spartan and needed a lick of paint. But it was no worse than most and the rent was reasonable. Dougie reckoned that the trainee salary on offer along with Marilyn's student grant would allow them to live reasonably well. They put an offer in. Marilyn would get half of the deposit money from her family and Dougie would pay the other from the deposit he would get back from the Haringey landlord on Monday.

Marilyn got a call from the Camden landlord on Saturday afternoon. Their offer was accepted. On Monday morning, when Dougie returned to the house for the last time, the roll he was on continued. There was a letter from the college. It was his exam results. He had passed all his subjects, three with distinction. His trainee position in the City was assured.

After a final look over the empty house, he locked the front door, and with a spring in his step, walked the short distance to the landlords' house which was on the street leading up to the main road.

After the "Ouija" night, the rationalist in Dougie was back to the fore. The whole Ouija Board experience he now attributed to autosuggestion stoked by the atmosphere combined with the dope, the alcohol, and the stress and strain induced by the exam season. No, all was still well in a materialist world.

He was met at the landlords' house by his daughter, Despina, a beautiful looking girl about twenty, with long, dark hair, green eyes and an olive, clear skin. He had met her on a few occasions where she often translated for her father when his English failed him. She'd often been the topic of admiration, even drooling, in the house. But even Steve accepted that to make a move would be potentially fatal in the close-knit Haringey Greek-Cypriot community.

Despina invited him into the gaily decorated front room and apologized that her father was detained elsewhere but she had his deposit money for him. This was how it was with both father and daughter: quick and business like. She brought out a brown envelope from a drawer by the bay window and took out some notes. After counting the amount of his deposit, she handed the cash to him which he put in his pocket.

'I trust your stay was pleasant,' she said to him.

'Yes, indeed,' he replied, having no intention of mentioning the strange experiences which he now put down to tricks of the mind.

'Good, thank you.' That was it, time for him to go. He went towards the hall when he suddenly realized he really needed the loo. It was a thirty minutes' walk to Marilyn in Holloway with no facilities enroute, so he really needed to go.

'Forgive me, but could I use your bathroom?'

'Of course,' she replied. 'It is upstairs, the first door at the top.'

'Thanks.'

He went upstairs noticing the array of sepia tinged photographs on the walls as he ascended displaying what he assumed were family portraits or scenes from their native Cyprus. Leaving the bathroom he noticed a large picture of three men on a fishing quay, some boats in a harbour, and hills in the background. He got to a third of the way down the stairs when he stopped. It felt like a thunderclap had broken over him and he swayed slightly on the staircase, needing to hold onto the banister.

At the foot of the steps, Despina had noticed his shock; his face had become chalk white. 'Are you all right?'

Dougie didn't answer her immediately but moved back up to the landing, studying the picture intensively. Two of the three men in the picture were crouching at the quayside, wearing sweaters, and holding onto a rope attached to the boat. The third man was standing. He was tall and although the picture was in black and white, he could discern that the coat he wore was dark, possibly green coloured. Most significantly for Dougie was the man's eyes; they were bright and piercing, almost sparkling.

Dougie was mesmerized, his mind constantly switching between the "spectre" at the foot of his bed the previous February and the man in the picture. They were one and the same.

In an almost hoarse, strained voice, he asked Despina, who was now beside him at the top of the stairs: 'Who is this?' pointing at the tall man.

'Why,' she immediately asked. Turning to her, he noticed she was frowning.

'I thought I recognized him from somewhere.'

'That's impossible. He's been dead for twenty-five years,' she said decisively.

'Sorry, of course, he looks like someone I met once.' He sounded unconvincing, even to himself.

Despina made to go back down the stairs. Dougie continued to stare at the picture. 'Who was he? The tall man?'

She turned round. The frown was now almost a scowl. 'My uncle.'

'How did he die?'

She came back up to him. 'Why do you want to know this?' There was now an alarmed look in her eyes.

Dougie decided to be straight with her. 'I'm really sorry but a couple of months ago I thought I saw a...oh God, how could I put this? I thought I saw a vision of someone like your uncle in my room.'

'What do you mean a vision?'

'Well, you know, just a fleeting vision.'

'Like a ghost?'

'You used the word, but yes I suppose that's what I mean.'

'How often did you see it?'

'Just the once, as I say. But then...' He broke off, unsure whether to continue. He decided that since he'd started, he may as well get it all out. '...And then a few weeks ago, the boys and I decided to use this Ouija Board and it spelt out a name, and the name said that it hated someone. When we asked it to name who it hated, it started spelling out D followed by an O, and I freaked.'

'What was the name it spelt?'

'Costa, followed by the number 9.'

It was the girl's turn to turn completely white. 'Are *you* all right?' Dougie asked.

Her eyes were wide open staring at the picture. She spoke very softly, almost inaudibly. 'My uncle's name was Costa.'

It was like another thunderclap had broken around him. 'Jesus!' was the only reply he could muster. They stood in silence for a few minutes until Dougie asked once more: 'How did he die?'

She turned to face him. 'I will tell you, but then you must leave and, please, never tell anyone else.'

'Sure.'

She turned back to face the picture. 'The man on the left kneeling down is my father. This picture was taken some time in the mid-1950s in Cyprus. Both my father and my uncle came to England in 1957. Both opened shops in Green Lanes. My father bought this house and my uncle the house you lived in.'

Dougie's eyes opened wide. Despina continued: 'My father's business was successful whereas my uncles was not. He got into debt. My father offered to help, but he felt ashamed and refused. Eventually, he went bankrupt. This was many years before I was born, you see. My father bought the house from him, but he just could not get over the shame of coming over here and failing, or this is what my family tell me only a few years ago. So, one day he took his own life.'

'How?'

'He took a rope and hung himself.'

'Where?'

The girl looked straight at him. 'In a room in the house you stayed in.'

'Which room?' Dougie knew the answer before she told him.'

'The front room facing the street.'

'That's the room I was in,' he said in a hushed tone.

'I know,' she replied, equally hushed. 'We have had reports over the years about appearances in that room, but my father ordered us to say nothing in case we frightened people, and no one would take the room.'

'I can understand that. Just one final question, if I may. What year did he die, if you know?'

'It was two years after they moved to England. 1959.'

Dougie could hear a key in the front door. Despina was alarmed. 'That is my father. You must go!'

They went down the stairs and reached the bottom as the door opened and Dougie recognized the father, a small muscular man, slightly overweight, with dark receding hair. Despina spoke rapidly to him in Greek. The man smiled and offered a hand to Dougie which he took. It was a firm grip.

'I told him you had a pleasant time staying in the house,' she said. The man went into the living room. 'Now, please, never speak of what I have told you.' She urged him.

'I promise I won't.'

He left the house, the door shutting behind him. It was a bright afternoon. The sun was out now, burning off the earlier clouds, making it quite warm as he strode up the street, turning into the bustling Green Lanes. As he glided through the busy street, almost on autopilot, making his way to Holloway, his stream of consciousness was consumed by alternating images of Despina's uncle at the quayside with his brother; the "spectre" of the same uncle at the foot of his bed; the terror of the Ouija night; and the horrific "vision" of Costa dangling from a rope with a broken neck in the room Dougie had slept in for six months.

Dougie's world was turning on that Monday afternoon. Where was the rationality, the scientific objectivity in any of this? he mused.

All was definitely not well in the material world.

Johnny Dialectic and the Shakespeare Enigma

By Henry Buchanan

He lost it the night of his 'Stratford debate'
When Kay and her brother came with worldly mate –
Cousin to a duchess, sussed, chilled and suavish,
Dauntless connoisseur of the finest hashish.
"The Shakespeare plays were written by a writer,"
All three concurred, high on Earl Grey and pipes,
"A Cambridge man who's altogether brighter
Than Stratford Will's professorial hypes:
A scientist, philosopher, and scholar –
An opium-taker high in the state –
A well-placed eye on the Good and the Great –
On Francis Bacon, sir, we'll bet a dollar.
Shaxper did props for the Lord Chamberlain's Men,
A 'front' who Latin Classics would never ken."

But well-*fou* Johnny defendeth the bard
As "working-class bloke" who worked "awful" hard:

"This aristocratic conspiracy

To claim him for your selves is piracy,"

He slurred, with snarly stare at dopey dude,

"Upper-class twit, I'll smack you on the nose!"

Pin-drop silence, they got up in sour mood.

"Bacon's *Plantations* is *Tempest* in prose,

We feel sorry for chaps who self-delude.

Another time we'll Shakespeare praise or cuss;

Your bevvy, man, has 'witched this frightful fuss."

To door they went, sweet Kay livid and brood.

"Marx liked Shaxper," she whined, "and Bacon too.

Dumb dialectics have got hold on you!"

Links:

https://brill.com/view/journals/djir/23/1/article-p105_011.xml

The Outing

By Anne Ferguson

It had been Robert's idea. He was the youngest of the three boys but he was the leader, the one who always had some scheme in hand and today was no different.

"Och, it's too nice a day to go to school. Let's go somewhere, do something a bit more exciting." He surveyed his two companions knowing that they would agree. They always agreed with him.

"Aye", said Michael. "That wid be great. Sure, it wid Tam?"

Thomas, however, remained silent. This did not indicate dissent but merely reflected the fact that Thomas seldom spoke.

"So, we're agreed then. Good."

Robert grinned in appreciation at the two brothers. He was a democratic leader, and it was important to him that his decisions were met with approval. Most of his classmates couldn't understand why a bright lad like him hung around with the two McCann brothers. After all, the boys didn't even attend their school but went to the "special" school further down the street. Robert didn't care what others thought. He liked the fact that there were never any confrontations with the two brothers. Both boys were always happy to fall in with all his plans.

"Right. Let's go then.", he said brightly and set off at a brisk pace. The brothers followed on behind him.

"Where ur we goin'?" asked Michael as he tried to draw level with Robert. Thomas kept to his usual position, bringing up the rear.

"The station."

"Aw great! Ah love trains so ah dae. Hear that, Tam? We're goin' tae the station so we ur."

Thomas plodded on doggedly behind them seemingly totally unconcerned.

"Tam loves trains an' aw," Michael felt obliged to inform Robert.

They were now approaching the "Cross", leaving behind the derelict landscape of partially boarded up tenements set amidst the areas of demolition. The streets here were busier, brighter, and noisier. Thomas drew closer to his companions. Most of the passers-by paid little attention to the boys, they were too busy trying to get to work. Some people did look at them, their attention perhaps caught by the rather incongruous appearance of the threesome; the small, stocky, smartly dressed figure in front, wearing a wide grin on his broad, pale freckled face which was topped by a thatch of carrot-red hair; behind him the two thinner, taller figures with blank grey faces and wearing shabby, somewhat grubby clothes. Only Robert was aware of those who glanced at them. He rewarded them with one of his infectious grins so that, as they went on their way, they too had smiles on their faces.

The boys continued their journey past the carpet factory where Robert's mother worked.

"See my mother's factory," indicating it as he spoke, "it's built like a palace in Venice."

"Venice?" queried Michael.

"Yes. Venice. It's a place in Italy, where the people travel about in wee boats instead of cars."

"How?"

"Because they've got lots of canals there instead of streets."

"What's a canal?"

"It's like a river only it's been built by men," Robert explained patiently." Anyway, in Venice there's this big fancy palace and when they built the factory here the men decided to copy it. That's why it looks so different from all the other factories around here."

"How come you know everything?" asked Michael, looking duly impressed.

"S' easy. The teacher was telling the class about it just last week. She showed us photos and stuff. Do you not get things like that in your school?"

Michael looked puzzled and thought for a moment before replying.

"Ah don't 'hink so." He looked towards his brother for confirmation, but none was forthcoming. Thomas had remained oblivious to their conversation.

By now the surroundings were becoming less familiar to the two older boys but Robert was still striding confidently onwards. The boys trotted alongside, having complete trust in their leader, until eventually they reached Saltmarket. A certain look of recognition swept across Michael's face.

"Ah know where ah'm ur noo!" he declared. "This is the toon!"

Robert nodded his assent and continued to lead the way along the crowded pavement. They turned a corner into a quieter street which in turn led to a large square.

"Hey Rab, we've been here afore. Sure we hiv?"

"You're right Michael. We came to see the Christmas lights. Remember?"

"Aye," his friend replied, his face lighting up at the memory," Ah mind it noo. It wis great so it wis. Ah love Christmas so ah dae."

They crossed the Square and were soon in the station where Robert examined the destinations board.

"Aberdeen," he read aloud. He pondered. "No, too far away. Stirling. Maybe. It's not too far and it's got a castle. Edinburgh. Yes, let's go to Edinburgh. It's got a castle too."

He looked at his friends to see if they were in favour, but both were gazing in fascination at the trains. He nudged Michael and tried again.

"Do you fancy going to Edinburgh? We could visit the castle and....."

"Ur we really goin' oan a train? Ur we gonnae see a castle an' aw?"

Michael couldn't believe it. This was turning out to be one of their best days ever.

"Let's get some sweeties for the journey. How much money have you two got?"

The boys produced some coins from their pockets and handed them to Robert. He added their copper coins to his silver ones and then headed off to the kiosk. The others followed. The woman behind the counter frowned at their approach and watched warily as the boys ran their eyes over the display of confectionery. Undeterred, Robert gave her a friendly smile.

"Me and my pals want to buy some sweeties for the train. We're going to Edinburgh for the day." He then turned to his companions.

"Have you decided yet what you want?" he asked.

The boys indicated their favourites only to be informed by Robert that their finances didn't stretch that far.

"You'll have to choose smaller packets. Besides you'll get more sweets for your money if you buy these." and he indicated the cheaper sweets at the front. "We can afford to buy quite a few packets then. It's better value. Isn't that right Missus?"

The woman found that she was smiling despite herself.

"Thank you very much," he said giving her yet another big smile as the transaction was completed.

Robert moved a short distance away from the counter and then proceeded to divide up the sweets equally between the three of them, although most of the money had come from his own pocket.

"Your train will be leavin' in a few minutes son. Ye'll need to hurry if you don't want to miss it."

"Thanks missus." shouted Robert over his shoulder as he started to run in the direction of their platform, followed by his friends and by the woman's friendly gaze.

Robert was by nature an honest boy, but his high moral stance did not extend to the area of fare-dodging. He did not see this as a crime, merely a necessity if he wanted to broaden his horizons. Several of his friends had been on the receiving end of one of his lectures when they had admitted to shoplifting or pinching from their mothers' purses. However, on the subject of travelling without a ticket on public transport, Robert remained silent, his philosophy being that you weren't really hurting anyone. It was this belief that now enabled him to slip past the ticket collector guilt-free.

The guard was moving down the platform checking that all the doors were closed. The three boys hurled themselves through the nearest of the few doors which remained open and heard it slammed shut behind them. Robert led his friends into the compartment and within seconds the whistle sounded, and they were off!

Once seated, Michael and Thomas concentrated on their sweets while Robert surveyed his fellow passengers. By now the rush hour was over and their compartment reflected this. A middle-aged woman was ensconced diagonally opposite and seemed intent on her newspaper. She had glanced at the boys as they collapsed into their seats, but Robert's warm smile had failed to melt her frosty expression. Further up the compartment a young couple sat entwined and had eyes only for each other. Robert was used to this scene, having seen it enacted by his teenage sisters and their succession of boyfriends, but he still did not appreciate it.

"Oh yuck!" he thought. "How can people be so soppy?"

He returned his attention to Michael and Thomas who were still captivated by the landscape outside, a landscape considered to be rather dull by regular commuters. Unlike his two friends Robert had made this journey before and was therefore less impressed. He began to think about school. The class would be doing their maths by now. He smiled. All things considered he was happy to be sitting on the train. Maths was his least favourite subject, but he did feel a tinge of regret at missing Language, especially today when they were going to be writing a story. He started to compose a story in his head but did not get very far before he was interrupted.

"Hey Rab! This is magic so it is. Look at the fields. They're dead green so they ur. D'ye think we'll see coos an' that?"

"Maybe a bit further on Michael."

"D'ye hear that, Tam? We'll mebbe see coos Rab says."

Thomas made a completely unintelligible reply due to having a mouthful of sweets. He continued to stare out of the window.

Their journey continued mainly in silence broken occasionally by the rustle of sweet wrappers, exclamations from Michael and explanations from Robert. By the time the train reached Falkirk the pile of sweets had been replaced by a pile of scrap paper. Robert collected all the pieces and put them into the largest packet. He couldn't abide mess. He then examined his hands.

"I'm going to the toilet to wash my hands. They're all sticky."

"Ah'm comin' wi' ye. Ah'm needin' the toilet. Tam! Are you needin'?

Thomas responded with a shake of his head.

"Wait here for us." Robert instructed. "We'll not be long."

Thomas turned from the window and watched them go.

"We'll need to wait till the train's left the station before you can go." said Robert as they made their way up the aisle.

"How?"

Robert explained the reason to Michael in graphic detail with a look of relish on his face. This contrasted with the look of disgust on Michael's face.

"That's boggin' so it is."

They had only been gone a few minutes when Thomas decided to go after them. He trundled off in the direction they had taken and met his two companions as they made their way back to the compartment. Robert gave him instructions as to where the toilet was located.

"Will you be alright?" asked Robert. "Do you want one of us to come with you?"

"Naw. He can go by hissel'. Sure ye can?" Michael enquired confidently of his brother. His faith was rewarded by a nod of Thomas' head.

Thus assured, the two boys continued their way back to their seats, leaving Thomas heading off in the opposite direction.

Michael installed himself at the window once more and Robert sat alongside him.

"Are you sure Tam will be okay?"

"Aye."

Both boys went on to discuss how they would spend the time in Edinburgh. Michael was delighted to hear their first stop would be the castle. Robert once again passed on to Michael the information that he considered important.

"You'll really like it. It's on top of this big rock that used to be a volcano. It's got cannons and they fire one of them every day."

"For why? Is it no' awfy dangerous?"

"No. It's just to let folk know the time." Robert turned and looked down the aisle.

"How? Hiv they no' goat any clocks therr?"

"Of course, they have. It's just a tradition. They fire it at twelve o'clock. No, I mean one o'clock." Robert turned back to face his friend.

"But ur we gonnae see it?"

"And hear it!"

They spent a few minutes discussing how close to the gun they would get and the best way to protect their ears, if the noise was as loud as they were expecting. During this conversation, however, Robert had seemed somewhat distracted.

"Thomas is taking an awful long time at the toilet."

"Aye. Wir mammy gets right angry wi' him sometimes cause naebody else can get in. He goat locked in wan time an' ma da hid tae climb up a ladder tae get in the windae an' unlock the door."

Both boys laughed at the picture this created. Mr. McCann was a very large man and the window in question was quite small. Robert suddenly became more serious again.

"All the same, I think we should make sure he's alright."

Robert stood up and then turned to his friend who remained seated.

"Are you not coming? He is your brother after all and you know your mother tells you to look after him."

With a sigh Michael rose from the seat and both boys set off in the direction of the toilets once again.

"Whit'll we dae if he's locked in? Hey Rab whit'll we dae?"

Robert made no reply but quickened his stride and both boys disappeared out of the compartment.

It was quite some time before the two of them returned and Robert looked somewhat anxious. They resumed their seats but Robert seemed unable to settle. He kept leaning out and looking up and down the aisle. The woman with the newspaper looked over at him but, when Robert returned her gaze, she quickly returned to her crossword. Robert continued to look at her, but it became obvious she was determined to avoid any eye contact with him. Her body language left him in no doubt that she was not going to become involved with their problem. He shifted in his seat and again began to look up and down the aisle but to no avail. No-one else appeared. Michael's interest in the views from the window seemed to have waned, for he kept turning and looking hopefully at Robert.

"D'ye 'hink he's awright?" he kept asking.

"Yes. I'm sure he'll be fine." came the reply but each time sounding slightly less confident.

At last the train drew into Waverley Station and, apart from the foolhardy, macho types who chose to alight while the train was still in motion, the boys were the first to descend. Robert rushed along the platform with Michael in his wake, only stopping when he saw someone in the familiar uniform of a British Rail employee.

"Excuse me Mister."

The man turned round and looked down at Robert, with a friendly expression.

"How can I help you son?"

"I've got a problem. It's my friend. He's got lost."

The porter, noticing Michael arriving at Robert's side, looking somewhat puzzled. He looked from one to the other and was about to speak when Robert interjected.

"No. Not him. It's my other pal, Thomas. He was on the train with us but he's disappeared."

"An' ma mammy's gonnae kill me. Ah'm supposed tae mind oot fur him so ahm ur."

"He's Michael's brother." Robert explained.

"I see." the man responded, "There were three of you on the train."

"Aye"

"But then Thomas went off to the toilet and he never came back. Me and Michael went to look for him but we couldn't find him."

"I'm sure he'll be on the train somewhere. Let's go and look."

The two boys looked at each other and then back at the man.

"Honest mister. We looked everywhere but he wasn't there."

"Rab 'hinks he fell oot."

At first the man thought that the boys were having a joke but, looking at their faces, he was sure that they really believed that this was indeed what happened to their friend. He tried to reassure them and insisted they go back on the train.

"He's probably still on the train wondering where you two have gone to."

Robert and Michael looked doubtful but decided to prove their point by returning with him to the train, where there would be no sign of Thomas. Of that they were sure. After a thorough search of every compartment and every toilet, the porter had to agree. Thomas was definitely not on the train.

"When was the last time you actually saw him?" he asked.

"When he went to the toilet."

"But what makes you think he's fallen out of the train?"

"Because, when we went to look for him, the carriage door near the toilet was open."

"Surely you don't think your friend opened the wrong door."

A look of incredulity spread across the man's face so that Robert felt obliged to explain.

"Well, you see, Thomas is different. He's a bit," and he paused while he tried to find a tactful way of putting it. "Slow."

"Aye an ahm the wan who's tae look oot fur him so ahm ur. He's no' very good on his ain so he's no. Ahm the smart wan in the family so ahm ur. That's whit ma mammy says."

By now the porter had realised that he was not going to be able to solve this problem on his own.

"Come on boys. I think we'd better go and see the police about this."

At the mention of police, a wail came from Michael.

"Naw. No' the polis. Ma da tellt me if ah got intae bother again he'd gie me a doin' so he wid."

"It's alright son. You're not in any trouble but they can help us find your brother."

"Besides," added Robert helpfully, "The police here won't know you like the ones in Glasgow do. And anyway, it's part of their job to find missing people. Isn't that right Mister?"

Robert's confidence was by now virtually restored. He had always had complete trust in those in uniforms.

"Yes son, that's right," said the porter and he then turned to Michael and laid a comforting hand on his shoulder.

"Don't you worry. They'll soon find your brother."

He was relieved to see that Michael appeared to calm down, but his own feelings were ones of concern. If Robert's theory was correct, and he was beginning to believe it was, then what injuries might Thomas have incurred falling from the moving train? He gave an involuntary shudder which was observed by Robert.

"Are you alright Mister?"

The man looked down at the concerned face of the small boy and gave him a reassuring smile.

"Of course, I am. Right. Here we are."

"Railway Police" read the inscription on the door that they were about to enter.

Once inside the porter gave a brief resume of what had taken place since the boys had approached him. The looks of disbelief that met the tale were like his own expression when he had first been told.

"I'm convinced that they're telling the truth."

One of the policemen came over to the two boys. Michael tried to shrink behind Robert but was unsuccessful in his attempt due to being several inches taller.

"Hello boys. I'm P.C. Boyd. What are your names?"

Robert could feel Michael's hands gripping onto the back of his sweater as he answered for both of them.

"Right lads. Let's sit down here and you can tell me everything you can."

As the boys moved over to sit at the desk indicated, the porter bade them farewell explaining he would have to get back to work.

"You know where to find me if you need me," he said to the constable. "The wee red-haired fella is your best bet," he added quietly. The constable nodded and went to join the boys at the desk.

"Right boys. Just a few details. Could you give me your full names and your pal's as well."

"Robert George Smith."

P.C. Boyd then looked at Michael who was becoming more apprehensive by the minute.

"Go on. Tell the policeman," whispered Robert in encouragement.

"Michael," he said, pausing before he nervously added, "McCann."

"And your friend's name?" P.C. Boyd directed this to Robert.

"Thomas McCann."

"So Michael. You're Thomas's big brother?"

Michael forgot his apprehension as he hastened to correct the constable's mistake.

"Naw ahm urnae. He's older not me so he is."

Robert intervened and explained that Thomas was the oldest of the three boys.

"Thomas is eleven. Michael is nine and I'm going to be nine in five weeks from now. Do you want our dates of birth? It's okay Michael, I know yours and Thomas's."

Robert knew dates of birth were beyond his friend's ability.

Robert then went on to tell in detail all that had happened from the time he and Michael had met Thomas on his way to the toilet, right up until they had spoken to the porter.

"Have you any idea of where the train was at the time you saw Thomas going to the toilet?"

"It was just after it left Falkirk station because me and Michael were going to the toilet while the train was stopped there."

"Aye. But we didnae dae nuthin'till it went oot the station. Sure we didnae?"

Michael looked anxiously at Robert for corroboration unsure of what punishment was meted out to those who failed to ignore that instruction.

P.C. Boyd suppressed a smile and assured them that if Thomas had indeed fallen out at that point, then it should be relatively easy to find him. He proceeded to make a phone call, explaining that he was contacting the police in Falkirk. On replacing the receiver, he told the boys that the police there were going to search along the railway line leading from the station in the direction of Edinburgh.

"They'll ring us whenever they've got any news. So now we just have to wait. Would you like something to eat?"

"Yes please," said Robert.

"What about you Michael?"

Michael nodded warily. He wasn't accustomed to hospitality being shown by policemen, but his face lost its worried expression when a tray was set before them, bearing two mugs of Irn Bru and a plate of biscuits.

"Thank you very much," said Robert ever mindful of his manners. He used his elbow to remind Michael of his.

"Whit the...Oh. Aye. Ta. This is great intit? Ginger. An' choccy biscuits. Ma favourite." And he selected one from the plate.

"P.P.P. Pick up a Penguin." Robert did his penguin impersonation, aware of the fact it was less impressive when he was sitting down, but Michael laughed anyway.

"Ah love Irn Bru an aw. Mind ah think ah like Tizer better."

Again, he felt Robert's elbow and saw his look of disapproval.

"Naw. Ah do like the Irn Bru jist as much so ah do. Hey Rab it's a pity Tam's no here. He'd fair enjoy this so he wid."

Robert was aware of the absurdity of this remark but showed solidarity with his friend by agreeing.

"There's one thing puzzling me." P.C. Boyd interrupted their munching and slurping. "Why did you not pull the emergency cord?"

Not wanting to display a mouth full of chewed up biscuit, Robert waited for a moment, swallowed, and answered.

"I thought about it but I was worried in case we got fined. You see we haven't got any money."

"But you don't get fined if it's a real emergency."

"I wasn't sure if it was."

P.C. Boyd shook his head. "Well then, why didn't you tell someone on the train?"

"I looked for a guard or someone in a uniform but I couldn't see anyone. Then I was going to tell this old lady but she didn't want to speak to us. She just kept reading her paper.

Further discussion was halted by the sound of the phone. Robert tried to follow the conversation but as all that was being said at their end was along the lines of "Hmm,I see", "Uh huh"and "Right. O.K." he was none the wiser. Michael meanwhile was unwrapping his fourth "Penguin".

"That was the Falkirk police. They've found Thomas."

"Is he alright?"

"Yes. He was lucky. He landed on the grassy embankment and the train must still have been travelling quite slowly. They think he's got a broken arm and he'll probably have a few bruises but, apart from that, he appears to be fine."

"Thank God!" Robert exclaimed and felt a sense of relief. The outing had been his idea after all, and he felt guilty about not taking better care of Thomas. He took his position as leader very seriously.

"D'ye hear that, Michael. He's okay."

"Does that mean we can go and see the castle noo an' the guns an' that?"

Robert remained silent being unsure of what was to happen next, although he was quite sure that it wouldn't be a visit to the castle. P.C. Boyd intervened.

"Your brother's being taken to hospital in Falkirk. We're going to take you there."

Although Michael was eager to see his brother, he could not hide the disappointment he felt at not visiting the castle. Robert saw his friend's crestfallen expression.

"We'll go to the castle another time."

Michael found some solace in this promise and in the fact that they would be travelling to the hospital in a police car. The policeman who was to take them, promised that he would turn on the siren for them when they reached a quiet stretch of open road.

Half an hour later they reached the hospital and the boys were happily reunited. The members of the medical staff were also delighted that now they would get the information that their records required. Thomas had only been able to provide his name and the fact that he came "fae Brigton".

X-rays had revealed that Thomas had indeed broken his left arm.

"You'll be able to get your friends to sign your plaster when it's dry," a nurse commented with a smile.

While they waited one of the policemen wandered off and returned with drinks and crisps which the boys tucked into once they had expressed their gratitude, prompted of course by Robert. Warning glances to Michael ensured there would be no complaints about the flavour of the crisps.

The boys were taken back to Glasgow by car.

"It's alright boys. We'll explain everything to your mums and dads. It wasn't your fault, Thomas. They'll understand."

The brothers sat on each side of Robert and were true to form gazing out in fascination from the car. Robert was employed in creating a story in his head. From time to time, he responded to the friendly remarks of the policeman. He had decided he would give up his ambition to be an astronaut like Neil Armstrong in favour of being a policeman - a detective. In his story he was solving the mystery of a headless corpse found in the River Clyde.

"Look!" exclaimed Michael. Is that no' the hospital ower there?"

"Yes. That's the Royal Infirmary. And the Cathedral."

They pulled up outside the McCann's close with the boarded-up windows on either side. The boys got out of the car and one of the policemen accompanied them to the close mouth.

"Ur ye comin' wi' us Rab?" Michael enquired.

"No, you're alright. I'll just go home."

"Are you sure you don't want one of us to come with you son?

"No thank you. I'll be fine. I'm just round the corner."

"It wis a great day so it wis."

"Sorry we didn't get to the castle, Michael."

"S'awright. We seen it so we did fae the car on the way tae the hospital tae get Tam. He had a great time an aw. Sure ye did?"

"Aye. Rerr." Thomas rewarded Robert with a smile.

The brothers, accompanied by the constable, disappeared into the close and headed upstairs to their flat.

Robert reached his own close. His house would be empty. He wanted to tell someone about his day, but he knew that when his sisters came in, they would have no time for him. By the time his mother arrived home she was always too tired to be bothered with him. As she busied herself in the kitchen his chatter was usually greeted with "Give me peace Robert. You're doing' ma heid in."

He wondered what it would have been like if his father hadn't left. He imagined him and his dad sitting there, swapping stories, and sharing jokes. He could only vaguely remember what his dad looked like. His mother had put any photographs well out of sight.

Robert gave a wistful sigh. "Still. There's always school tomorrow."

He imagined the reactions of his fellow pupils when they heard about his adventures. The teacher would go through the motions of scolding him. But Robert knew she enjoyed his tales as much as his classmates.

Smiling again, he reached inside the neck of his shirt and pulled out the string from which his key dangled. He unlocked the door and went inside.

The Final Chapter

By Jonny Aitken

Sirens shriek on barren streets,

Gloved civilians gawk and wince,

Their body language tense,

No longer a bestselling thriller,

These books have no pages left,

The final chapters written by another author,

More akin to a dystopian horror,

Orwell would be proud,

Or maybe he's just laughing in his grave.

Tinker, Tailor, Shepherd's Pie.

By Hugh V. McLachlan

From the instant I first saw him, I disliked the man. He stood out of the rain under a tree talking to Victor in Barshaw Park in Paisley. As I approached, the pair broke off their conversation and I overheard the stranger say: 'See you in the gym, Vic'.

'See you in the gym, George', replied Victor.

As he hobbled off into the depths of the park with a huge, bedraggled dog as his reluctant companion, he said: 'Don't Welsh on your debts, Vic.'

'I didn't realise that you went to a gym', I said to Victor.

'I don't', he said. 'Neither does George. His remark was ironic gallows humour. He is very ill. Or so he says'.

I said nothing. Victor continued: 'Believe it or not, people used sometimes to say, when taking leave of someone "See you later, alligator" and the person to whom this remark had been made would say in response "In a while, crocodile".'

I was not sure whether to believe him. You never could be sure with Victor. He is quite a joker. For instance, I once said that someone or other was 'pissed as a newt' and Victor said that he was very surprised to hear me, of all people, using such a derogatory expression. I was baffled. Then he said that the expression was very insulting to Eskimos. He said that it arose from the observation that Eskimos were particularly prone to getting drunk – not surprising, he said, since there was not much else to do if you were snowed into your igloo for long periods of time. 'Pissed as an Inuit' was the original expression, he said, but it became corrupted and abbreviated into 'Pissed as a newt'.

I was mortified. I resolved never to use the expression again. However, the smiles of Victor and our mutual friend, James Warren soon blossomed into laughter and I realised that, once again, Victor had extracted the urine – taken the piss – out of me.

On the other hand, sometimes, he could surprise you by saying something that sounded like it was only a joke but was actually true and even made you think in a different way about things. For instance, when Alex Salmond lost the referendum in 2014 and cancelled a celebratory party he had organised to follow the declaration of the result, I said that this was 'sour grapes'. Victor said it was no such thing. He told me about Aesop's fables. One was about a fox who was very keen to eat some grapes that were high on a particular vine. The fox tried all day as hard as it could to reach the grapes, was unable to do so and decided to give up. However, the fox became aware that his antics had attracted an audience. So, when he walked away, he tried to hide his inadequacy and failure from them by saying: 'I don't actually want the grapes anymore. That's why I have decided to give up trying to get them. They are probably sour'. This, Victor told me, is the origin of the expression 'sour grapes'.

Victor said: 'Alex Salmond did not pretend that he had not actually wanted to win the referendum. His mood was sour because he did not win it. This has nothing to do with sour grapes.'

We walked away from the park in the direction of Paisley Cross. I said: 'I don't remember ever before hearing any-one say: "See you later Alligator".'

'That shows how young you are', said Victor. 'It comes from a song by Bill Halley and the Comets called: "Rock Around the Clock". Notice the delicious ambiguity of the expression "around the clock". We do not always want to speak clearly or unequivocally'.

He started to sing 'Nellie the Elephant'. This might have been embarrassing if there had been more people around. 'An elephant', he said. 'And a trunk. The elephant packed her trunk and said "good-bye" to the circus. Delicious stuff.'

'It did not say "See you later, alligator"', I quickly pointed out. 'That might have made more sense in the circumstances'.

We stopped at the traffic lights on Arkelston Road even although the road was more or less clear. We could have made it, I am pretty sure. However, Victor is very cautious. He does not cross a road until the green man appears no matter how quiet the traffic is. Very strange.

'Who was that man you were talking to?', I said. 'I don't trust him'.

Victor smiled. 'George has that effect on people', he said. 'He gives the impression that he is always one foul away from a red card'.

It is interesting that Victor used such football imagery on this occasion. It is difficult to describe someone's face other than in very vague terms, but I can tell you reasonably accurately what Victor Tonkin looks like or looked like. When I first visited the home of James Warren, who is an Englishman and a mutual friend, I noticed a large poster of a smiling, handsome young man in a football strip holding a football. I exclaimed: 'Jesus, that's Victor when he was young'.

James laughed. 'Idiot!' he said. 'That's Bobby Moore'.

Bobby Moore was the captain of the English team long ago when they won the football World Cup in 1966.

When I saw Victor and George standing together in Barshaw Park it looked from a distance like Bobby Moore standing beside and towering over Jimmy Johnstone, had they both been alive at the time which, of course, they were not. Jimmy Johnstone, as every-one should know, was the dazzling, diminutive, red-headed winger who played for Celtic when they won the European Cup.

'He's a racist bastard', I said. 'George, I mean'.

'Racist?' said Victor. 'Why do you say that? You're so judgemental, so quick to condemn people harshly.'

'Because of what he said about Welsh people. He told you not to Welsh on your debts. What debts, by the way? It begs the question of your debts'.

'I'm glad that you said that it begs the question of my debts and not that it raises it. However, you are way off target with what you say about George and racism'.

I was puzzled, doubly puzzled. Then, I remembered that Victor had said before, several times in fact, that to beg a question is not the same as to raise a question, indeed, it is the opposite. For instance, if you say to someone 'Have you ever voted for the SNP?', you are raising the question of whether or not they have ever voted for the SNP. If you say to someone 'When did you stop voting for the SNP', you are begging the question of whether they have ever voted for them. You are implying that they have voted for the SNP and, therefore, that the question of whether they have ever done so has already been answered.

He told me the origin of the expression 'To welsh on your debts'. Victor is an academic. He is a bore at times. But not always. In the past, the jurisdiction of English civil and criminal laws did not apply in Wales. When people in England accumulated large debts, which they were reluctant to pay and their debtors were very keen to claim, they sometimes fled to Wales in order to avoid paying them. Hence, the expression 'To welsh on your debts' was not an insult to the Welsh'. It was, if you like, an insult to those who welshed on their debts, an insult they richly deserved. To call it a 'racist' expression is mistaken. So I was told by Victor. I believe him.

'George begged the question of your debts. I raise the question of your debts', I said. 'What debts?'

He seemed to be about to reply to my question when his attention was diverted towards Paisley Grammar School, which stood on our left-hand side as we walked along Glasgow Road. He had been a pupil there. A 'pupil', he would say: 'Not a "student" as pupils seem to be called nowadays. Is this some sort of misguided drive to try to eliminate distinctions and discrimination of any sort? Is it, somehow, all about inclusivity?'

Unlike Govan High, my former school, Paisley Grammar was a selective, fee-paying school when Victor was a pupil.

'I had mixed feelings about the place', said Victor, 'It was a rugby playing school then. I wanted to play football. We played football in the playground, of course, but never in the formal P.E. classes and there were no official school football teams.'

I had heard all this before, of course, but he went on to tell me things which were new to me. He left school abruptly near the beginning of his final, sixth year as soon as he received a letter to inform him that he had been awarded a place at Glasgow University on the strength of the Highers that he had gained the previous year. In mid-summer, several months after he left, he heard that an end of term football match between staff and pupils had been arranged. It took place somewhere in Hawkhead, I believe.

Such an event was a novelty for Paisley Grammar School. He went along to watch.

The centre-forward of the teacher's team was a P.E. teacher called Bob Scott. Despite a tendency to belt pupils harder than seemed justified to Victor and sometimes for behaviour which seemed to him to deserve no punishment at all, Victor respected and even liked the man as, it seemed, did most of the other pupils. He was silver-haired and stocky. He was not tall but was physically and emotionally tough. Very early in the match, Bob Scott and the goalkeeper of the pupils' team both ran – not terribly quickly - towards the ball near the edge of the penalty box. The goalkeeper, who was called Andrew Neil, picked up the ball comfortably. However, Bob Scott proceeded to jostle or pretend to jostle with the goalkeeper. Then, Bob Scott fell on the ground. He did not roll over. He remained motionless.

'Since the scene was comical rather than tragic in the eyes of the players and on-lookers, there was some laughter', said Victor. 'Someone - I can remember his name but I won't say who he was, not even after all these years - someone called out as Bob Scott lay there: "It's all right, he's only dead"'.

'And he was dead or very soon would be', said Victor.

'The game was restarted after a pupil who had been a spectator drove Bob Scott in the back of his small estate car to the R.A.I, the Royal Alexandra Infirmary as the local hospital was then called. The pupil was called Ian Noble and I am pretty sure his car was a green Morris' said Victor.

The game was still in progress when Ian Noble returned and solemnly told one of the teachers who was watching the game the grave news. The game was stopped. Players and spectators alike stood or shuffled around aimlessly, for a short time. 'One girl, she was called Margaret Hamilton', Victor said, 'Did an appropriate thing. It was, perhaps, the only fitting and proper thing than could be done. She was one of a group of athletes who had received specialist and, it appeared, much appreciated training from the dead man. She acted with maturity and sincerity.'

'What did she do? I asked.

'She wept bitterly, said Victor. 'She wailed loudly and long'.

I had recognised the name 'Andrew Neil'. Andrew, or Drew as he was more often called, was a photographer at The Paisley Daily Express where I was working at the time as a trainee reporter. Drew had a particular talent for taking aerial photographs many of which had appeared in the newspaper. They should put on an exhibition of them. I mentioned this to Victor.

'No', said Victor. 'The photographer you are talking about is Andrew Neil's nephew. The Andrew Neil I referred to, the goalkeeper in the match, used to be the editor of The Sunday Times. He also appears on politics programmes on the BBC. He was in my class at school. We were also friends at university. We were on the same course. However, I have not seen him for years. I knew Jim, his brother, better. I used to drink with him at the Lord Lounsdale Pub in Paisley'.

Victor drinks no more. I have known him only since he became and remained sober. Although Victor seems now to be a very peaceful and gentle person most of the time, he has a reputation for previous violent behaviour. To be more accurate, the reputation concerns talk of violence rather than particular violent behaviour of his that anyone can remember seeing. Apparently, when he got very drunk, he would talk about his part in the riot of the Glasgow Rangers fans when Rangers won the European Cup

Winners Cup. He would sometimes ramble drunkenly about the 'Battle of Barcelona' in which, as a youth, he fought hand to hand or, as he would put it 'Fist to face with Franco's fascist policemen…'.

Even more alarming and surprising, he would, when very, very drunk, seem to suggest that he might have killed or wanted to kill his first wife, who died in a car crash.

'You were in the same class at school as that old snob and wanker of a Tory?', I asked.

'I might even be slightly older than him, a few months, perhaps', said Victor.

'I don't believe it', I lied, unconvincingly.

'He wasn't a snob or a wanker when I knew him', said Victor. 'And, if he was a Tory, he was a strange sort of one. I remember that he was attracted to the Bow group, a think tank which was associated with the Conservative Party but in spirit and tone was, in my recollection, pretty similar to Tony Blair's later "New Labour".'

Victor continued: 'When I was young, I lived with my parents in a council semi in the Castle Policies, a housing scheme in Johnstone. When Andrew and I were both pupils at Paisley Grammar School, I remember visiting Andrew who lived in a similar council semi in Glenburn in Paisley.

'When he became successful, Andrew Neil created a registered company to process his earnings from various sources. It is called "Glenburn Enterprises Ltd". That suggests to me a sort of pride in and loyalty to his background, to his origins that I find admirable. No, I don't think of him as a snob or a wanker'.

Then, as we walked to the cross, past the Town Hall and statues of formerly famous rich Victorian businessmen, my friend reminisced further about his schooldays. He told the following story, which I found strangely unsettling. Was I listening to a joke or a confession? Or both? Or neither?

Victor and another boy were arguing about politics one day in a building in Paisley Grammar School. Victor chased the boy along a corridor towards a staircase, which the boy descended speedily. Whether this was done in a rage or in a jovial act of schoolboy horse play was not made clear to me. In a stupid act of juvenile recklessness, which he regretted immediately, he said, Victor threw his school bag down the stairs at the boy's head.

A frail old lady, a French teacher called 'Wee Alice', who had been recalled from her retirement to teach again at the school to ease the problem of a teacher-shortage, had been walking feebly towards the staircase. The boy brushed past her as the bag missed its target and landed with a thump at her feet. She shrieked and leapt to the side.

'It could', said Victor, 'have killed her. It could have done'.

'Who threw that bag?', Wee Alice said this to the boy.

'I do not know', he said.

'Who threw that bag?' Wee Alice repeated the question to the other schoolchildren who were at the scene.

'I do not know, Miss', said several voices.

Then, one of the schoolchildren suggested that Miss Young might open the school bag and, by looking at the name written on the books inside or on an attached label, discover the likely owner of the bag. She thought that that was an excellent idea but when she turned around to examine the school bag, both it and the schoolboy had vanished.

'So', said Victor theatrically, 'Take a bow and my grateful thanks, Andrew Neil. That quick-witted schoolboy and loyal friend was you'.

'How can we ever know what anyone else really thinks or feels?'

I was thinking more about George than about Andrew Neil when I said this. I was beginning to feel guilty about my prejudicial judgment of the man.

'There is body language but that can be very unreliable. And real language, too, but that can be even worse. People can deceive us deliberately or by mistake. We can deceive ourselves by stupidity or ignorance, for example'.

'We can rely on language, sometimes, on what people tell us about what they think and feel but even this can be very unreliable. People deceive us inadvertently. People deceive us deliberately or by mistake. Furthermore, we make mistakes when we try to interpret what other people mean by what they say', I said.

'Yes', said Victor, 'Local knowledge and context are often crucial in deciphering linguistic codes. For instance, "Yes" can sometimes mean "No" and vice versa. For instance, what does "Aye, right" mean?'

'I could not say. It all depends. Sometimes it means "Definitely not", which is the opposite of what it might be thought to seem to mean', I said.

'Quite', said Victor.

I said: 'And sometimes we say: "That will be right" when we mean "What you are saying is a pile of crap".'

'Suppose I said that we are going for the messages' said Victor.

Puzzled, I said 'We are going for the messages are we not?'

'Yes', said Victor 'But if someone overheard us who did not understand the local meaning of "going for the messages", he might think that we were clairvoyants, perhaps or couriers or secret agents of some sort'.

'Spot on', I said.

On my left-hand side stood Paisley Abbey when I said to Victor: 'I think I was a bit unkind to George'.

'Possibly', he said.

'He was actually telling me one of his stories just before you arrived'.

George, so Victor told me, had been visiting his son, who works in Dubai. He was sitting in a lounge at Heathrow on his journey home when he got into conversation with a woman, who was mopping the floor. She asked him where he had been. He told her of his son's job, his son's salary, his son's fabulous apartment, his son's clever children and his son's wonderful wife. His visit lasted over a month, he said.

She repeatedly said, 'Oh, that's fascinating, tell me more' as George described his holiday.

'The more she said this' said George, 'the more I began to think that there was a very faint rasp in her voice which was just the same as my wife had in the early stages of her illness. The cancer that killed her. If she had been diagnosed then, they might have saved her, they said.

'I was thinking of how I could tactfully suggest that she should see a doctor', said George to Victor.

'I said to her: "There is a very delicate matter I would like to raise with you"'.

'Don't bother trying to beg me from me', said the woman. 'I don't believe a single word you say. The next time you tell someone a cock and bull story about a long and luxurious holiday in a hot country with your rich and highly talented family, don't forget to get yourself a tan first'.

'I was shocked. "Cheeky bastard", I thought to myself', said George to Victor.

'There's a history of skin cancer in my family. Even in Paisley, I keep out of the sun'.

I said to Victor, 'What did he say to the woman about her voice?'

'Yes', said Victor, 'I asked him that question.

'Oh', said George to Victor, 'I said nothing. It was none of my business. Probably only a cold or some other minor condition, in any case'.

'Dear oh dear. You're a bastard, George', I thought to myself. 'Straight red card. Off!'.

Publications by **Hugh V. McLachlan** include the following books in the areas of the history of Scottish witchcraft, medical ethics and social philosophy:

Larner, C. J., Lee, C. H. and McLachlan, H. V. (1977) *A Source-Book of Scottish Witchcraft*, University of Glasgow, 1977; reprinted, with a new preface by McLachlan, The Grimsay Press, 2005.

McLachlan, Hugh V. (2005) *Social Justice, Human Rights and Public Policy*, Humming Earth, Glasgow.

McLachlan, Hugh V. (2006) *The Kirk, Satan and Salem: The History of the Witches of Renfrewshire*, (editor), The Grimsay Press, Glasgow.

McLachlan, Hugh V. and Swales, J. Kim (2007) *From the Womb to the Tomb: Issues in Medical Ethics*, Humming Earth, Glasgow.

He has written also written numerous academic and journalistic articles. See, for instance:

http://scholar.google.co.uk/scholar?hl=en&as_sdt=0%2C5&q=H.V.Mc Lachlan&oq=h

https://philpeople.org/profiles/hugh-v-mclachlan

https://www.opendemocracy.net/en/author/hugh-mclachlan/

https://philarchive.org/rec/MCLNTS

https://diametros.uj.edu.pl/index.php/diametros/article/view/415

https://link.springer.com/article/10.1007/s11673-021-10091-6

Hugh.McLachlan1@ntlworld.com

The Pie-eyed Piper

by Lizzie A.

Hamelin was a German town, near a riverbank –
a plague of rats then came along, so that the whole town stank!
The rats they scuttled everywhere – up trouser legs – in hats -
up sleeves of jumpers, inside shoes and in domestic cats!
They raided pantries, ate ice-cream – drank soup straight from the ladles,
put on nightdresses, striped pyjamas and slept in kiddies' cradles.
Those rats they grew so big, so fat, so crafty and so strong
and folk put clothes pegs on their noses - to combat the big "pong"!
The townsfolk they became upset and marched to the Town Hall
"Do we pay taxes for velvet robes and **you** to have a ball?"
they screamed at the Mayor, and then began to shout –
"Do something about this plague of rats – or we will kick you out!"

The Mayor and his councillors sat down to make a plan.
They heard a tap upon their door and in came a weird man –
thin as a rake, with an old robe, half yellow and half red –
he looked as if his wife had simply kicked him out of bed!
"**I** am the Pie-eyed Piper and, although I look quite funny,
I'll rid your town of all the rats -if you give me loadsa money!
For a thousand guilders I'll play my pipes and the rats will disappear –
"We'll give you fifty thousand", said the Mayor, "**and** more beer!"

The Piper smiled a little smile and lifted pipes to lips –
he shimmie-shammied forward and girated his slim hips.
A strange noise was soon to be heard, a rumble and a grumble –
then out of all the houses all the rats began to tumble!

The music from the Piper's magic pipes, the rats did haunt –
some of them looked mesmerised, while others they looked
gaunt.
Out filed rats of every age, colour, shape and size -
young and old, black and white, with straight and squinty eyes!!
He led rats to the riverbank – parents, sisters, brothers
and all except for one did die – much faster than the others.
It returned to rat land and yelled, "Unpack all your luggage!
Don't go to Hamelin 'cos the music there is rubbish!"

The folk of Hamelin celebrated - bells rang, steeples rocked –
then up stepped the Piper and the Mayor looked real shocked!
"My fifty thousand guilders!" said the Piper, "if you please!"
"The rats they are all dead now," laughed the Mayor, "so - **hard
cheese!"**
"Don't fool with me!" the Piper snapped "Make sure you pay me
soon –
or I will seek revenge by playing a very different tune!"

The Mayor and his Councillor were a really cheeky pair -
"Play your pipes until you burst – and see how much we care!"

The Piper stepped into the street and played a little ditty
a pattering of feet was heard – Joseph, Mary, Kitty.
Then all the children followed, they ran, they skipped, they
hopped
and when they reached the riverbank, the parents' hearts all
stopped!
They gave huge sighs of sheer relief when the Piper turned
and led them to the mountain – but, then, their stomachs
churned!
On one side of the mountain, opened a great door -
the kids danced in, the door it shut, the kids were seen no more!

The folk of Hamelin wept - then laughed - the teachers, joiners, fitters -
'cos now they could "go out" at night – without paying babysitters!

Lizzie Allan (A 'revolting rhyme'.)

"MAKIN IT ON MY OWN": FROM NURSE TO RADIO PRESENTER.

By Rosalyn Barclay

Rosemary has been a radio presenter on a voluntary community radio station, Camglen, in Rutherglen since March 2015. Rosemary started being a radio presenter before she retired from nursing in 2017. She worked in various roles in nursing starting with student nurse followed by a staff nurse, student midwife, staff midwife and finally a practice nurse.

How did it all start for Rosemary? She was listening to online radio on a cold, wintery night in December 2014, had a " light bulb moment " and decided she wanted to be a radio presenter with no experience! She applied to 3 radio stations – Camglen, Sunny Govan and the hospital radio at the Victoria Infirmary. The only one that replied was Camglen radio.

Camglen Radio started about 15 years ago in Aran Towers in Cambuslang where they had a month's licence to broadcast every few months. Some of the current presenters started broadcasting there. Then they got a 5-year licence and needed presenters, both experienced and non-experienced. They moved to the premises on the corner of Farmeloan road and Main Street in Rutherglen in March 2015 before moving to the current studio at Number 18, Farmeloan road, situated across from Chapman's bar. The studio is situated on the top floor of the building which was an old church hall. On the ground floor is a cafe and kitchen with a meeting room. On the first floor, is a huge space with great acoustics. This is used for various activities, including film shows and can be hired for any type of celebrations.

She received an e mail inviting her in for an interview and was very surprised. A few weeks later she went in for an interview with the Head of Volunteers and, very surprisingly, she was asked back that night to start her training. Rosemary was shocked but excited too to learn all about radio.

Three hours later Rosemary returned and met the other prospective presenters. She was the only lady there! Rosemary was surprised to see the studio; it was a "box " in the middle of a large room. Rosemary was expecting a studio similar to what she had seen on television, a large studio with large decks. No, it was much smaller with a strong sound-proofed door, a small deck, 2 chairs and a small table and no room to swing a cat in. Outside the box was an office area where the presenters could prepare their shows or drink a coffee made in the kitchen along the corridor. Also, along the corridor were meeting rooms. A few weeks later, after she had completed her training, Rosemary was offered a show on Sunday afternoon from 1 to 2 pm. She was delighted and she started her show the week of the launch in the new premises. At first, Rosemary played music she had at home and often had a theme – all girl singers, singers from round the world or singers whose names started with the letters of the alphabet. Nowadays, she plays music sent to her from all the world and CDs she buys or sent to her by singers from all over the world. She has listeners all over the world and listeners tune in at the time or listen after the show.

Since she started, she has interviewed artists from all over the world – live in the studio and also by phone. During Covid-19 she did many Zoom interviews. They have been from countries as varied as Hong Kong, Australia, Cyprus, India and the US.

Since Rosemary started her show she has visited many

venues in the city and further afield, some of which she didn't know existed . A venue close to her is The Glad Cafe in Shawlands which hosts many events, including gigs. The venue is situated at the back of the building. At the front is a cafe / bar serving foods with a twist …

The Glad Cafe has an interesting history. In days gone by, it was a bakery. In 1840, it was established by Neale Thomson of Camphill, a local philanthropist, who undertook to provide his workers with nutritional food and also improved their working conditions. He lived in Queens Park in a large house which is now flats. Neale was born in Camphill in 1807. His father died in 1831, then his two brothers in 1833 and 1843; then the family business, Adelphi Cotton Works in Hutcheson, fell into Neal's hands.

He became known for the care of his workforce, introducing shorter working hours before a law was passed on working hours. Neale also encouraged his workers to open a savings account and he matched their contributions. In the bakery, good quality bread could be bought more cheaply than in other shops. Many other branches opened in the city and queues formed before the delivery vans arrived. In 1855 he commissioned Alex Greek Thomson to build terraced houses for his workforce in Baker Street near the bakery; by 1964 only one remained which was demolished in the 1970s.

Rosemary's nursing career started in 1971. In those days the training took place in a hospital and lectures were held in the school of nursing; nowadays it is a 3- or 4-year nursing degree at a university. Rosemary trained in the Western Infirmary in Glasgow. Her first day memories are as clear as a bell. The student nurses gathered in the grounds of Knightswood hospital with their parents or whoever came with them. They were a bunch of fresh-faced girls and one boy, which was unusual in those days, as men usually did psychiatric nursing. Rosemary remembered one nurse who stood out from the rest as being very beautiful with long dark hair and beautifully dressed. Later she found out that she was half German and until recently ran her late husband's jewellery shop in the north of Glasgow.

The nursing course lasted 3 years and the lectures were held in the new school of nursing at Gartnavel general hospital. Rosemary and her nursing colleagues were provided with a coach to take them from their accommodation to the lectures. This lasted a few weeks until some nurses would turn up late then they had to get a normal bus to lectures.

When Rosemary was in first year, she developed meningococcal septicaemia – a rare illness. At the time, all the nurses in her class were tested and one was found to be a carrier. Rosemary was admitted to Ruchill infectious diseases hospital as was the nurse who was the carrier, although Rosemary didn't know that at the time. Her parents were called by the Matron and were asked if they were sitting down as she was going to tell them that their daughter was unwell. Sadly, they were due to go on holiday to Switzerland and had to cancel. On their way to visit her they saw an advertising board saying, "Nurse seriously ill in hospital". What a shock that was to them!

Rosemary was treated with intravenous antibiotics after a lumbar puncture confirmed it was meningococcal septicaemia. The only lasting side effect she had was a tint scar on her left wrist.

She was so lucky that when she became unwell, she was transferred to the Sick Bay where the Home Sister (who had been a Fever's Nurse) knew what she had and got help quickly. The symptoms were a severe headache, nausea and then a rash on her arms. Rosemary was in hospital for 10 days and after a few days rest at home she returned to her training.

It was quite an achievement for Rosemary to reach 100 shows. She said to herself "how did that happen?" Then, when she hit 200, it was another milestone and after that she stopped counting.

On her 100th show, it was a packed hour with a band and a guest. The band were Pronto Mama who she had seen a few months previously at a Celtic Connections event at the Centre for Contemporary arts in Glasgow`s Sauchiehall Street. It was a recording for Janis Forsyth`s radio show and the late Rab Noakes was also on that show.

Rosemary had on her show the fellow radio presenter, Ronnie McGhie. He is a presenter at Pulse radio in Barrhead, formerly at Irvine Beat Radio. They met through their common bond of being Radio Presenters and often meet up for lunch or a drink in their favourite city centre venue, Champagne Central, a bar in the Central Station where they discuss new music they`ve heard They like to people watch from the window looking onto the concourse of Central Station. It was a fun packed show.

Her 200th show was memorable too with 2 guests on who were singers and authors and good friends. They were Ian Donaldson, former singer with H20. Rosemary had seen him on Top of the Pops when she was a teenager and never dreamt she would have him on her show 40 years later. H20 had 2 top-ten hits with "I dream to sleep" being the most well-known. It was number 17 in the music charts of June 1983. Ian went solo and brought out a CD in 2018; the title was "From stars we came", celebrating his return to music and he played 2 packed gigs to celebrate the launch. His debut novel was published in 2016, entitled "A Rainbow in the Attic". She meant to ask where he got the idea from as it is about fairies and people write about what they know about. He has a second book in the pipeline.

Her other guest was T.R. Scott, known as Tam. He is a singer-songwriter and author too. They had great fun, chatting, discussing their books and eating the 200th show cake! Ian and Tam have known each other for many years since meeting in Kelvingrove Park in 1981. Tam's book is called "Being Boiled", an autobiographical story of growing up in the 70and 80s in a rough area of Glasgow and how he escaped to avoid getting involved in the troubles. He did that with the aid of music. His second book is in the pipeline too which Rosemary is looking forward to reading.

But the biggest coincidence of all was that Rosemary noticed in Tam's book that he mentioned Duncan McKay who played with the band Steve Harley and Cockney Rebel from 1975 to 1977. Duncan is an online friend of Rosemary. He's a singer, arranger and keyboard player who has recorded 8 solo albums and collaborated with many artists, including Kate Bush and 10cc.

Rosemary had many guests on her radio show both for interviews and live sets before Covid hit and the studio shut down for two and half years. The guests were from all over the world, including Ireland, Hong Kong, Sweden, Scotland and America.

Her first guests were the singers who wrote the introduction to her book, Jamie McGeechan and Graham Marshall.

Jamie was Rosemary's first live act on her show. He sang a few songs. Jamie sings under the name Little Fire which is the meaning of the boy's name Aiden who happens to be his little brother – 21 years younger than him. Instead of a normal 21st birthday present he got a wee brother! Little Fire's repertoire varies from his own songs to the songs of Robert Burns. He is the only artist to record an album of Robert Burn's songs in Robert Burn's cottage.in Alloway in Ayrshire. He has also performed with many artists including Damien Rice and Joan Armatrading. His last CD was titled "Midnight Kingdom" and was about his long-distance love with his now American wife, Sara. Jamie has also written a book called "GLAIKIT" comprising of Scottish language poems. In September 2020 it was number one in Amazon's bestselling Scots e-book category.

He is a passionate Scot who now lives in America with a love for music writing and communication. When he lived in Scotland he wrote for the local newspapers, the Ayrshire Post and the American Scottish foundation.

The other early guest on Rosemary's show was Graham Marshall whose song is her show title and also her book title. He was originally from Linwood before travelling the world and settling on the east coast but now lives in Manchester. Graham made a prize-winning video when he went busking from John O` Groats to Lands' End, covering 1500 miles and singing at 18 different places. It is called

"Out in the cold". Rosemary was delighted that he sang a few songs, including "'Makin it on my own".

Another guest she had on singing live was a singer from Hong Kong but originally from Ayrshire. Samuel Barbour was on her show in August 2019 while he was holidaying in Scotland with his wife and daughter. He is a teacher of English to primary school children and his nickname is Teacher Ham, given to him by a pupil.

Samuel started playing the guitar aged 11 taught by his father, then he studied classical guitar and furthered his education at Edinburgh's Napier University. As a teenager he played in various venues and a variety of music. Rosemary enjoyed Samuel's repertoire of songs including "California Dreaming" which has been used to advertise Scotland's new NC 500 known as Scotland's route 66. It is a scenic 516-mile route around the north of Scotland, taking between 5 and 7 days to drive it. It is advisable to visit in May or October, as most restaurants, attractions and places to stay are open. It has been voted one of the world`s top coastal touring routes.

Her greatest honour was having a musician from Ireland on her show that she has followed for several years. Jack Lukeman is a singer songwriter from Athy in Co. Kildare. His real name is Sean Loughman, and he was born on 13th

February 1973. She first heard him singing on You Tube with another Irish singer, Camille O Sullivan, performing "Fairy Tale of New York", originally written by Jem Finer and Shane McGowan in 1987 and sung by many artists.

Rosemary`s friends thought that she was a mad groupie until they heard him, and some liked him and some didn't. He has released 17 CDs and written over 100 songs. He has a massive following worldwide and has toured with many artists including Jools Holland, The Proclaimers and Imelda May.

Rosalyn has a novel "Was it worth it", under the name Annie Frances Fisher, published on Lulu, and another "Making it on my own" available by contacting her directly at
rosalyn_barclay@yahoo.co.uk

The Accidental Genius (my part in his success)

By Frank Chambers

There's nothing more satisfying when you're a teacher, than to hear that one of your former charges is making their way in the world and doing well for themself. It's always something to talk about when the girls meet for coffee. I would like to tell you about Gordon MacGregor, a former pupil of mine and the exception to the rule.

It all started with the 4th year maths exam. An unremarkable, bog-standard test. What could go wrong?

Question five was the cause of the trouble and it set in motion a most unfortunate chain of events.

The question read. $1.7-3x = 2.6$. Find x?

A basic equation, appropriate level of difficulty for the class, I was not anticipating any problems. Why should I, I had been using the same test paper for the past five years.

Anyway. When I came to mark MacGregor's paper, it went like this.

Question one, zero out of three.

Question two, zero out of two.

Question three... one out of five.

Question four... zero out of three. Honestly! He couldn't count two elephants in a telephone box.

Then I got to question 5. Well, right away I could see there was no working, which is never a good sign. I assumed the bold Gordon had just missed that question out. I wasn't surprised. Decimals AND negative numbers, it was just too much like hard work. I glanced at the box where the final answer should have been written, poised to put a big red score across it, when I noticed something was scribbled at the side. I took a closer look. It was an arrow that pointed to the x in the question. Next to the arrow the bold Gordon had written, "Here it is."

Oh, very funny!

I should have just marked it zero out of three and left it at that. Stupidly, I decided to tackle him. Next time he was in my class I showed him the paper and asked, "What's the meaning of this?"

"Meaning of what, Miss?" says he.

"Don't what Miss me," I barked, prodding the paper with an angry finger. "This here."

He shrugged his shoulders and boldly stated. "The question said find x, so I found it."

"Are you trying to be funny?"

"No Miss," he smirked.

I told him. "You're not even original. That joke is as old as the hills. You've got zero for the question and I'm deducting three marks from the total for your cheek". And that was that, as far as I was concerned.

Next day the headmaster is up at my door. "Mrs MacGregor has been on the phone," he says. "The woman is extremely upset. Something about you deducting marks from Gordon's test paper."

"I did", I said, and retrieved the offending paper from the pile on my desk. "Look at his answer to Question five."

He studies the paper... for a lot longer than I thought was necessary. He scratches his chin, then adjusts his spectacles. He shifts his weight from one leg to the other, then shifts it back again. His bottom lip starts to protrude, and his head starts nodding up and down. Eventually he turns to me and says, "The question is a bit ambiguous."

"What do you mean, ambiguous?"

"Well, find x?" he says. "Would it not have been clearer if the question had read, something like work out what number x must be."

"Are you joking?" I said. "That's how it is put in all the textbooks and that's what has been in exam papers since I was a pupil. It's a perfectly valid question."

"Well, I'm afraid others may not agree," says he. "You had better give him the marks. His mother could take it to the Education Department, and I don't think either of us want that. Do we?"

I knew he was referring to the recent stink generated by the gender-neutral toilets. I said nothing, just closed my eyes and shook my head, but deep down I knew he was right. If it went to Head Office, they were sure to cave in. I should have given him the three marks for the question and reinstated the three marks deducted for his cheek. It would still only have given the boy 15%. Stupidly, I said I would re-word the question and let him sit it again.

"If you must," the Head says in that condescending tone. "We have to tread carefully here. You know, with his situation."

"His situation? I asked. What situation is that?"

"With the family belonging to a minority group."

"The MacGregors? A minority group? What do you mean?"

He looks left and right to make sure nobody is listening, then says in a whisper. "You know with the MacGregors being a travelling family."

I said, "A travelling family? What are you talking about?"

"Well, with them being travellers, gypsies, we have got to tread carefully. You must have noticed that the MacGregor children are always absent during the summer term."

I said, "Are you trying to say that the MacGregors are travellers?

"Yes, that's exactly what I'm saying."

"Because the family go to Glastonbury in a camper-van every year, it hardly makes them travellers." It was all I could do not to laugh. Middle class pseudo eco warriors would be a more accurate description. The parents had opened a vegan cafe and upcycling shop on the High Street and were doing very nicely thank you very much. Ms Crilley in the science department bought a set of garden chairs made from old tyres and got little change from five hundred pounds.

His Mightiness goes all serious on me and says, "There's a lot more to it than that Ms Rusedski. I know for a fact that Gordon goes up north to pick raspberries during the picking season. He gave me a very nice photograph to prove it."

"Was that after you had queried his attendance record by any chance?" I got no answer, just the "how dare you" stare.

I wasn't prepared to let it go. "The photograph?" I enquired. "Did he tear it from the front of his maths folder by any chance? The one of him standing next to a caravan eating something from a cardboard box?"

"Yes, that sounds like the one. Blairgowrie in Perthshire, I believe."

That's not Blairgowrie, I said. It's not even Perthshire. That's the chippy van the pupils sneak off to at lunch time. I know that picture. If you look carefully, you can just make out the high flats on Hillfoot Street in the background. And before you ask, it's Nico DiRosa that owns that van. He was a pupil here, before your time, and the DiRosas are most definitely not travellers. The family have owned the cafe at the Cross since before the war.

"Well, I don't know about that," says he, looking a wee bit flustered. "The important thing is, if the MacGregors identify as travellers we have no alternative but to accept it. Are you certain that's a chip van in the picture?"

"One hundred percent," I say. "You can check for yourself. It hides behind the chicken factory."

"Oh, don't mention the chicken factory," he says. "That's a problem I could have done without."

Now, Baillie's Chunky Chickens is the biggest employer in the town and half the parents in the school work there. I feared the worst. "Don't tell me the factory's closing?" I ask.

"Closing! No such luck. They're expanding and have just announced a hundred new jobs."

Well, I thought that was marvellous news, we might get some of the Christmas leavers a job. I was more than a bit confused though, by the negative tone. I was soon to be enlightened.

"I thought you would be pleased", I said. "Its great news for the school. Isn't it?"

"If only life were that simple Ms Rusedski. We have a quarter of the pupils eligible for free school meals, it's taken me two years to get all the parents registered. If they start getting jobs in the factory, we could end up with hardly anyone qualifying for free dinners."

"I still don't see the problem," I said.

He gave me one of those pitying looks. A look that said, "not future management material". "The deprivation coefficient, Ms Rusedski." I shrugged my shoulders. "It will go down." Again, I shrugged. I could see the exasperation building up on the man's face before he barked at me.

"A high deprivation coefficient is our only hope of getting the school out of the failing category. If we don't have enough free dinners, we are sunk."

"I see." I was a little bit hurt by his assessment. The raising attainment committee, of which I was a member, had come up with a plan to boost results and therefore get the school out of the failing category. The plan was already being implemented with the current first year. I pointed out this fact.

"Even if your initiatives work Ms Rusedski, it will be another four years before we see any results. We can't wait that long."

We? What he meant was *he* couldn't wait that long. So that's how it is, I thought.

Sandy had never been in any post for more than three years. It was now two and a half years since his appointment as Head Teacher. Evidently, he was eyeing up his next career move. Director of Education perhaps, the exam board or something in the private sector. Who knows?

The Head made to leave, but then stopped, scratched his chin and said: "I am glad we had this little chat. You have given me an idea. We may be out of the failing category sooner than you think." With that he turned and left.

Anyway, to get back to Gordon MacGregor. I rewrote the question. $1.7-3x = 2.6$. EVALUATE x. I was quite pleased with that one. I got him to re-sit the question the next time he was in my class.

No arrows this time. No, just a paragraph of text. Oh aye, I thought, and started to read.

"X has many VALUABLE uses. It can be a signature for people who can't write. It is good for indicating where something is, as in X marks the spot. When you vote in an election you use an x." He finishes by saying: "It is also used a lot in maths equations."

Well, I wasn't accepting that, especially the last bit, it proved he understood the original question perfectly well. Proof he was at it.

I went straight down to the Head's office clutching the evidence in my hand. His secretary said, "I'm sorry Jean, Sandy is unavailable. He's interviewing for the new Head of Diversity at the moment. The woman could see that I was not happy and asked, "What's the matter? You look a bit agitated."

I said, "It's that damn Gordon MacGregor in the fourth year. His Mightiness has got it into his head that he's a suppressed minority, so he gets away with bloody murder. I'm down to show him this latest bit of cheek."

"I know what you mean," the secretary says. "You're not the first member of staff to be down complaining about that one. But before you go any further, can I tell you that the Head has just submitted an application for special funding, so the school can better meet the needs of travelling people.

"Meet his needs?" I ask. "It's a bloody good kick up the backside he needs." My non p.c. language was overlooked, and the secretary continued.

"He's got a brother and two sisters in the school, plus eight cousins. If the application is successful, the school could get an extra £60,000 a year." She paused for a moment, to let that little nugget sink in. "Not only that Jean, but if the school is recognised as having exceptional educational needs we will no longer be considered as failing."

Those two revelations took the wind right out my sails. £60,000 of extra funding is not to be sneezed at. And to be no longer in the category of failing school, well that would mean no surprise classroom visits, no crisis meetings after hours and, best of all, we might be spared the Head's excruciating motivational talks."

I went straight back to my room and marked the question 3 out of 3, reinstated the marks deducted for cheek and thought no more about it.

Over the next two years, a half dozen other families were persuaded that they too were travellers, and the school duly enjoyed the perks. Funding increased and not only were we taken out of the failing category, but we had started to climb further up the council's league table.... once "exceptional circumstances" had been taken into account. Exam results were no better, but everybody was happy.

The week before prize giving in MacGregor's 6th year, a memo was sent round asking staff if there was anything special they wanted included in the Head Teachers address. Stupidly, I thought I would have a little joke. I was sure Sandy would see the funny side. Before I left that night, I penned a wee note and dropped it into the Head's pigeonhole.

It read. "Re prize giving. Gordon MacGregor, who will be leaving us this year, is without doubt the most original mathematical thinker the school has ever produced. His insights on the subject have challenged conventional wisdom and led his teachers to reassess their practice. We owe him an enormous debt of gratitude." A private joke between two colleagues, that was all it was meant to be.

Unbeknown to me, His Mightiness was scheduled to be away the week of the prize giving, lecturing at a conference of head teachers on how to turn round a failing school, would you believe. He had handed over responsibility for the ceremony to the new deputy, who had only been with us for two months. Let's be kind and say the woman was still finding her feet. So far, she had mastered keeping a seat warm.

Anyway, the poor woman thinks she has found the highlight of her speech. Not only that, but she also has a brain wave and decides to create a special prize for the occasion and, wait for it, invites the press.

Well, with the school now regarded a beacon of excellence, if you are daft enough to believe the hype, it was not just the local paper that turned up, some of the nationals were also represented.

Being the last week in June, the MacGregor family had already left for their annual round of music festivals and Hippy gatherings. They could not be contacted. The star attraction would not be present to accept his special award. The hapless Deputy Head had to pacify the assembled posse of reporters, who were none too pleased that there would be no photo opportunity. She gave them a load of flannel about respecting the traditions of travelling people and that she fully understood why Gordon could not attend the ceremony. The motley crew didn't believe a word, but they still had a good story.

Next day's headlines: "Traveller pupil is mathematical genius." In the absence of Gordon or his parents to interview, the press just made stuff up. Mad crazy stuff linking the MacGregors with pearl fishing, magic potions, and the gift of second sight. Luckily for me it was the last day of term, and I didn't have to face the music.

It didn't end there, however. One of the Sundays got in on the act and did a full page spread in its education section the following weekend. Still no sign of the MacGregors, but the Head had been contacted by that time and had evidently decided it was in his best interest to perpetuate the myth, though he deftly shifted responsibility for any quotes to the maths department. He couldn't resist however pontificating on the ground-breaking work the school was pioneering with those marginalised by society. The picture of Gordon and the chip van accompanied the article. The Head must have provided it himself, but not before he cut out the sight of the high flats.

I don't mind telling you it was the worst summer holiday I have ever had. Every time the phone rang, I nearly jumped out my skin. I dared not look at a newspaper in case my name was splashed across the front page. I was dreading the start of the new term.

Walking through the gate on the first day back, I'm expecting to be summoned to the Head's office. And was he not lying in wait for me, just inside the main entrance?

"Ms Rusedski, I'm glad I caught you. Could you come along to my office for a moment. With that he turned and led the way, me following behind like the naughty schoolgirl. He lets me into his office, asks me to take a seat, but leaves the door open. It's going to be a public beating, I thought. The two secretaries in the outer office were already shuffling their chairs into position to get a good view.

I considered denying it was me that wrote the note, I never signed the thing after all. Then I remembered he would recognise my handwriting. I was about to demand that my union rep be present when he passes over a cheque and says, "What do you think of that?

The only thing I took in was that the cheque was for ten thousand pounds. I thought, if I'm sacked for gross misconduct and lose my registration, I'll never be able to work as a teacher again. Ten thousand pounds is not going to last long. I couldn't think straight. Couldn't decide whether to beg that he reconsider his decision or just tell him to stick his job.

"Ms Rusedski, what's the matter, you look disappointed. There's a letter too." He hands it over to me. "And Mr Pollock is here from the Herald to take your picture."

I turned round and there's a photographer standing in the doorway holding up his camera. Behind him is the entire management team and all the office workers, every one of them sporting a grin like a Cheshire cat.

"What do I do here?" I asked myself. The humiliation was bad enough already, there was no way I was going to be subjected to any further ridicule by letting them plaster my picture across the bloody newspapers.

"There will be no pictures," I insisted, and readied myself for charging through the lot of them to make my escape. Then the Deputy who had organised the Prize Giving chips in her tuppence worth.

"Jean. It's not every day that the school wins such a prestigious award." The Head then adds: "Ten thousand pounds for the Mathematics department will be very welcome I'm sure."

Only then did I look properly at the letter. THE MATHEMATICAL SOCIETY OF AMERICA, it said, International Award for the Promotion Of Excellence. My wee joke had crossed the Atlantic.

Further than that, as it happened. Letters of support had come in from the four corners of the globe and there were invitations to talk at conferences the length of the country. I refused to go to any of them of course, but there was no shortage of volunteers ready to take my place.

The MacGregors had been completely oblivious to all the attention they had been receiving. It was their practice to go completely off grid during their annual summer odyssey. No phones, no computers, no newspapers and no access to social media. When the family finally returned home at the end of August, they were dumbfounded to discover they had become celebrities.

Gordon took it all in his stride and milked the situation for all his worth. In an interview on local radio, he told the presenter that he was torn between an academic career and one in the arts. By arts he meant Electrogrind music. His parents also realised that they were on to a good thing and said nothing to rock the boat. The vegan cafe, elevated to "restaurant" in the papers, was featured on the TV news where the pair proudly proclaimed that all the "positive vibes" surrounding their gifted son had been good for business.

Come October things had settled down. The ten thousand pounds was all gone, but every pupil had a brand new maths textbook and the department had pens and pencils aplenty. Gordon MacGregor had been pushed to the back of my mind.

Then one Monday morning, just before the interval, I get this phone call from a Terence Fitzwilliam at some obscure college of Cambridge University. "It's concerning a former pupil of yours, Gordon MacGregor."

"How can I help you?" I ask.

"The boy has no mathematical aptitude whatsoever."

"I could have told you that," I said.

"He couldn't count two pheasants on the master's dinner plate."

"Again, I could have told you that."

"Did you not claim that he was a mathematical genius, the most original thinker the school has ever produced."

"Did you not look at his exam results?" I responded.

"He said in his application that he was always travelling during the exam diet."

"Isn't there some sort of entrance test for such circumstances?" I asked.

"There is, but that was during his travelling time, and he couldn't attend."

"An interview?"

There was an embarrassed silence before the man continued. "Cancelled at the last minute."

I finished the sentence for him. "Because he was travelling!"

"Yes."

"So, you let him in to one of the most prestigious universities in the world on the strength of a few newspaper headlines?"

"The college prides itself on its initiatives to embrace diversity and it is fully committed to widening access, while continuing to promote excellence." He sounded like he was reading from a brochure. "We thought we had found the perfect candidate."

"Do you mean you had quotas to fill?"

"I wouldn't put it quite so crudely, but some may interpret it in that way."

"I'm afraid you've been had," I told him. "If you want my advice, kick him out the door, tout suite."

"I'm afraid that is not going to be possible," the Professor groaned.

"Why not?" I asked.

"The Guardian has already printed an article on Mr MacGregor and now the Minister of Education has taken a keen interest in his progress. To top it all, a member of the royal family, who will be visiting the college next month, has explicitly asked to meet Gordon."

It reinforced my opinion that Gordon MacGregor was indeed a complete chancer. I repeated my advice that they should cut their losses and kick him out. I then bid the Professor good day and thought that an end of it.

Over the next couple of years even more parents in the school were encouraged to identify as members of a minority group, any minority group. It didn't matter which one, as long as it would qualify for "special consideration." Our coefficient for additional educational needs went up even further and the school, despite showing no improvement in academic standards, rose to the very top of the council's league table. There was so much extra funding sloshing about we were struggling to find ways to spend it. The classrooms all got re-painted in calming colours, perfectly serviceable books were thrown out and replaced with shiny new ones, the playing field got re-turfed, and iPads were stacked up like an Amazon warehouse on Black Friday. My suggestion that we should just hire more teachers was met with derision.

Things got to the ridiculous stage when a "laughing yoga" teacher was recruited, and the staff were all given a pass to the spa at a local hotel. I need hardly tell you I declined the services of both. With everything that was going on, Gordon MacGregor had been forgotten. That was about to change.

I was sitting in the staffroom all on my lonesome one afternoon. The other teachers on a free period were away getting an Indian head massage. Radio 4 was playing in the background, and I had poured myself a nice cup of tea and had a couple of custard creams at my side. The current affairs program was of little interest to me, they were discussing some upcoming bye-election in London. My attention was on my phone as I checked the weather forecast for the weekend.

I hear the name that sounded like Gordon MacGregor! Had I heard right? Surely not. I continued scouring the forecast for dry spells for when I could get out on my bike, but I'm now listening to the radio. The presenter is saying, "the twenty-year-old undergraduate would contest the Islington constituency." She continued, saying that "the student had been described by his old school as a "mathematical genius." A spray of tea and half chewed custard creams spluttered over the pile of jotters waiting for marking. The report went on to say that Mr MacGregor would quit University immediately in order to concentrate on winning the seat.

Right away I got on the phone to Professor Fitzwilliam. The man was as happy as a dog with two tails. After two and a half years of torment, he was off the hook. Gordon MacGregor was now someone else's problem. When the professor stopped laughing, he revealed that the college's token pleb had been allowed to defer sitting his first-year exams, due to his "special circumstances", and it was the same story with his second-year exams.

I said, "You couldn't throw him out because that would disappoint the Minister of Education and the Royal Family. Worse than that, you didn't want to risk the wrath of the Guardian readers. He had you right over a barrel."

The Professor replied. "You may think that, but I couldn't possibly comment."

I said no more. I could hardly take the moral high ground; I was in much the same boat myself.

Would you be surprised to learn that he won? At the age of twenty years, three hundred and twenty-nine days my former pupil became the youngest ever MP in the House of Commons, beating Mhairi Black's record by eight days.

His maiden speech was, ironically, on education. The honourable member gave an impassioned defence of the comprehensive system, crediting it with giving him his chance in life. Did Gordon actually believe what he was saying or was he just having a laugh? I honestly don't know.

The media loved him of course. How could they not with such a delicious back story. All the articles from the prize giving coverage were quickly rehashed but with arms and legs attached. The legend that was Gordon MacGregor became more and more fantastical with every new piece. One tabloid declared that when Gordon was growing up the family actually lived in the camper van, all six of them. The truth of the matter was that the camper van was a fully restored vintage VW that cost a fortune. When not pressed into service during pop festival season it sat in the driveway next to his father's Mercedes and his mother's Mini Clubman. The berry picking story was rolled out again complete with the bloody chip van picture.

Gordon became a regular on TV. "Have I Got News for You," "The Chase celebrity edition" and "Would I Lie To You," among others. He declined "I'm A Celebrity Get Me Out of Here," which, ironically, earned him plaudits for being a serious politician. "The Prime Minister has the Member for Islington on his radar", it said on Newsnight. The chancer could not put a foot wrong.

Back at the school the shit hit the fan when a real traveller family enrolled. They soon discovered there were no special policies in place to meet the needs of travelling people and the family were not slow in letting the Education Department know about it. The real travellers quickly moved on and the pretend travellers were exposed as frauds, along with the other minority groups the Head had invented. The extra points were removed, as was the funding, and the school was back in the failing category. The Head has been on "gardening leave" ever since, while the union fights his case. Other than that, everything was swept under the carpet, and nothing came out in the media.

Yet again I tried to put Gordon MacGregor to the back of my mind.

It was working fine until I switched on the news last night. First item, the Prime Minister's cabinet reshuffle. "It is widely tipped that a place will be found for rising star Gordon MacGregor as the PM seeks to inject new blood into a jaded looking cabinet." The "mathematical genius" quote was again repeated.

Needless to say, Gordon did make the cabinet. It was announced this morning. "Westminster's youngest MP, who is renowned for his exceptional ability with figures, has been appointed Chancellor of the Exchequer."

God help us all.

I'll need to leave it there, folks. I want to get to the bank before it closes, withdraw all my savings and change them into dollars. I suggest you do the same.

Novels by Frank Chambers

Lost on Main Street. https://www.amazon.co.uk/dp/B06XRYPZ9H

Busker of Buenos Aires. https://www.amazon.co.uk/dp/B09N8MZLSC

Music by Frank Chambers and Anna Chambers

Flying High. https://open.spotify.com/album/2j8n0Sq46odBk1XMSZCwZh

Are You Listening. https://open.spotify.com/album/5tDeRkc5b7lVxj5RSc2Fr1

The Belfast Belle.

By Duncan McDonald

Belfast. Harland & Wolff shipyard. 1975.

Maisie was the yard's newest and youngest cleaner. As a thirty-one year old single mum, being a cleaner didn't stop her from taking an interest in her appearance. Thus, she got the job of cleaning the new up market office complex. It comprised of four very plush offices. One for a bank of machines with multi-coloured lights, whirling tape decks and ticker tape spewing out everywhere. The snotty nosed staff called them "computers". They said the machines calculated the wages for the whole shipyard. What rubbish! How could half a dozen machines work out the wages of 5000 staff? The next office contained radio equipment to communicate with other shipyards throughout the whole world. These people watch too many episodes of Star Trek. The third room was a luxurious toilet complex - marble worktops, gleaming surfaces and expensive china fittings. If the hourly paid workers saw this, they would blow a fuse. Finally, the fourth office, this was the area Maisie was cleaning now. The entrance was labelled MICROFILM UNIT.

Maisie knew this was "the big new technology of the shipyard". This wasn't science fiction. Technicians had showed her how a thousand documents could be photographed and put on a negative, the size of a thumbnail. Right now, the technicians were working on the yard's archives. Two hundred years of files. A roomful of documents was being reduced to one box file.

Lunch break

It was 12 o'clock, so the technicians were heading to the social club for a liquid lunch. They would be at least an hour and a half, so Maisie would get peace right up to her finishing time at 2 o'clock. That was why she liked this job, she could easily pick up her son from the Primary school at 2.30, that and the good wage rates. Maisie worked 25 hours a week and earned the same money as her pals who worked 40 hours in bars and shops. The technicians didn't worry about leaving Maisie on her own because all H&W cleaners had a high security clearance. They could be working in sensitive or secret locations.

Secret file

Maisie started lifting files off a desk in order to clean it. She glanced at them with total disinterest. But one file stopped her in her tracks. It was labelled "Top Secret. HMS Belfast 1945. Compiled by Captain James Ridell and Petty Officer Brendan O'Hara. Not to be disclosed to general public until 1995." Brendan O'Hara was Maisie's dad.

HMS Belfast was the name of the ship her father served on during WW 2. Right up until his death in 1965 he never talked about his war experience, never talked about the Belfast.

Maisie opened the file and began to read.

"INCIDENT - North Sea – May 1940 - HMS Belfast".

4 months earlier.

Morning of Launch of HMS Belfast. Harland & Wolff shipyard, Jan 1940.

It was traditional for all British warships to be launched by minor nobility or a popular celebrity. Because of the war, warships were being launched ten a penny, so the yard management couldn't get such a person to launch the Belfast. The launch was due to begin at 2 o'clock that afternoon.

Present at the 9 o'clock emergency management meeting were all the ships officers and petty officers. Among them was Brendan O'Hara, chief engineering mechanic. The subject under discussion was who they could get at this late moment to launch the ship. No one could come up with a feasible solution. Petty Officer O'Hara tentatively addressed his Skipper. "Sir, there is one local celebrity who I know is available right now."

"Alright O'Hara," growled the Skipper. "Who are you talking about?"

O'Hara related to the group about a local theatre that all the crew frequented. The main compere and singer at the nightly shows was a local actress called Bernadette Brandon. Only twenty-one, but very popular locally. Bernadette also gave the Belfast's crew lots of attention, so she had become very popular with them. Thus, O'Hara was dispatched to persuade Miss Brandon if she would like to launch HMS Belfast. O'Hara was successful and reappeared a few hours later with the actress in tow.

It would be more accurate to say O'Hara was in tow. Bernadette swept into the shipyard. With her signature long red hair and jet-black hooded cloak with a blood red lining, she stood out among the grey flat crowds. Her personality stood out even more. She talked to everyone, thanked numerous people for letting her into their world-famous shipyard, then allowed senior naval officers to escort her up to the launching platform. An admiral passed her a note on what to say. Miss Brandon discreetly threw it away.

The tide was on the turn, so only minutes were left to begin the launch.

Bernadette took up the traditional position, bottle of champagne in hand. When the foreman shipwright gave her the nod, she swung the bottle hard against the ship's hull. At the same time, she bellowed "I name this ship HMS Belfast. God bless her and all the handsome young "Jack's " (sailors) who sail in her." The admiral frowned, but inwardly giggled. Seconds later the vessel plunged down the slipway and the Royal Navy had a new battle cruiser.

Bernadette was invited to a management cocktail party in the boardroom. She politely refused, saying she had to get back to the theatre for tonight's rehearsals. The extremely self-confident Bernadette never rehearsed. She had been invited to a knees-up the crew were having in the yard's social centre. For her it was a no-brainer, she knew where the most fun was to be had. She and the lads were not disappointed. Much singing and dancing was enjoyed by everyone. Bernadette made a point of giving out lots of promotional posters of herself and the theatre.

About six o'clock in the evening, the party started to break up. Bernadette had to get back to the theatre for the eight o'clock show. Many of the crew, including Brendan, promised they'd be there. Barely 10 minutes after she left, there was an unexpected air raid on the yard. Brendan reassured his young sailors there was nothing to worry about. "The Jerrys couldn't hit the side of a battleship with a hammer," he told them. They all giggled. Sure enough all the bombs missed the shipyard.

A couple of hours later all the off duty petty officers, including Brendan, marched off towards Bernadette's theatre. En route they discovered where all the bombs had landed. The street leading to the theatre was covered in debris and craters. Shivers ran up and down Brendan's spine. He took off at high speed towards the theatre with the others trailing behind. When he got near, he could see a dispersing crowd, no one was going in. At the entrance he recognized two older men. One was the theatre manager, the other was Mr. Brandon, Bernadette's father. He was holding a jet-black hooded cloak, with its blood red lining. Brendan's shivers turned to a stomach wrenching feeling. Worse than any he had felt at sea. Before he could talk to his seniors, nausea overcame him. He turned away from them and emptied the contents of his stomach into a nearby drain.

"Mr. Brandon, I'm...we are so sorry."

"A bomb exploded right next to her, Brendan," replied the manager. "She died instantly."

"A bomb, meant for the British, hit my wee girl," said Mr. Brandon angrily.

"I promise you Mr. Brandon," said Brendan. " The boys of the "Belfast" will never forget her."

"I know you are a good Derry boy, Brendan, but you keep those British boys away from me," he replied. With that he marched off, carrying Bernadette's cloak.

A week later was the funeral. Brendan, Captain Ridell, and some of the yard's management attended. Brendan kept the group, all dressed in civvies, to the rear of the crowd. He could just manage to see the expensive cloak being draped over the coffin. The Skipper asked if now was the time to go forward and pay their respects to the family. The Skipper never went out in Belfast town. He didn't have a clue about the underlying political and religious issues. Brendan decided now was not the time to give him a 500 year old history lesson. Instead, he said, "No sir, now is the time to return to the ship".

Back aboard the "Belfast" that night, Brendan put up Bernadette 's posters in key locations round the ship. He warned all members of the crew if they wanted good luck, they had to pat the poster and pay their respects to Bernadette. He thought how during the funeral, a number of locals had approached him, telling him how the Brandon family held the Royal Navy responsible for the starlet's death. Brendan didn't think the navy was responsible, he believed God was. He also believed God did things for a reason. There would be a reason for this tragic incident. Right now he didn't know what it was, but in four months' time, he would find out.

MAY 1940. Somewhere off the Scottish coast.

All the ship fitting work had been finished at Harland & Wolff. But, due to political issues, the shipyard was not allowed to fit any of the weapon systems. Thus, the Belfast was now transiting the North Sea en route to the Roysth naval base, for those systems to be fitted. She was totally defenceless. Captain James Ridell had been assured by Royal Navy Intelligence that there was absolutely no German activity predicted on his route. He was about to discover how wrong they were.

It was still very misty at 10 am of their second day into the voyage, when the Skipper heard the alarming shout from his best radar operator "Five unidentified vessels sir. Broad on the port beam. Small targets sir clustered together. Right on the limits of the radar sir, about 12 miles." The Skipper had a sick feeling in his stomach. He was pretty sure he knew what they were." Action stations, full speed ahead." he screamed. Sailors scurried about. Protective equipment was handed out. Klaxons and alarms sounded throughout the ship. Watertight doors and hatches were shut, not allowed to be opened until the danger had passed.

"Radio operator," shouted the Skipper. "Make to ASA (Admiralty Scottish Approaches). Our location, 5 unidentified vessels, 10 miles Northeast of my location. Can they identify? Use plain language." "Messenger. Find Petty Officer O'Hara. Tell him maximum revs. Our lives may depend on it."

"Aye Aye sir" he replied.

As soon as O'Hara got the message he visited the main engine compartments, tweaked and adjusted the control valves, advised his young mechanics how to handle their mechanical beasts. The last compartment he visited was the furthest aft, the main engine room. The last words he said to his five young operators, "hope you guys all paid your respects to Bernadette." In unison they all replied," of course boss." None of them had met Bernadette, but sailors were a superstitious bunch. O'Hara had all new crew members convinced that Bernadette was the most important asset the "Belfast" has. More important than the guns she was going to get fitted. As he left, the gas tight hatches were closed behind him and the air pressure in the compartment increased to one and half bar. This allowed the engines to develop maximum power. If the hatches were opened the air pressure would drop, causing the speed to drastically drop. Nobody, including O'Hara, would be allowed back in until the danger was over.

A few minutes after sending his message, the Radio Operator had his reply. "Admiralty has replied Sir he bellowed.

"Read it out loud," replied the Skipper casually from the bridge wing. He wasn't taking his eyes off the bearing of those radar targets.

"Vessels are unidentified and unauthorised. Intelligence reports 5 e-boats are missing from Bremerhaven (e-boats were the German equivalent of British fast torpedo boats).

No air cover available. Advise head due West. Firth of Forth gun emplacements will cover you when within range."

"Reply affirmative, Sparks."

"Helmsman, steer due west."

"Navigator, time till we're under Forth guns protection."

"Radar, give me an update."

"Do the blips match e-boat description?"

The Attack

The Radar operator was first to reply.

"Affirmative sir, definitely e-boats, changed course towards us. New ranges, Sir. Nearest vessel 6 miles, furthest 10 miles."

Six miles! The Skipper knew that the German navy had new torpedoes with a 5 miles range. The next voice he heard was the helmsman.

"Steady on two seven zero Sir."

Now the Navigators turn. "25 miles to the protected zone, if we can maintain maximum speed (35 knots), 40 minutes."

Then the lookout in the mast called through a voice pipe. "Shape coming out of the mist sir. Directly astern."

Ridell raced back to the bridge wing. As he put the binoculars to his eyes, numbers were tumbling through his head. He could outrun the faraway vessels but not the nearest one. His eyes confirmed all the previous bits of information. Definitely an e-boat. Then he saw puffs of smoke and quick flashes on either side of the vessel. Now the hydrophone operator was vying for his attention.

"Four splashes, directly astern."

The Skipper knew torpedoes had been launched straight at him. He shouted. "Radar, range? "

"Nearest vessel 5 miles sir," the operator replied.

That confirmed it, the e-boats had the new torpedoes. The e-boat Skipper had taken a risk. He had fired his full complement of torpedoes at maximum range. But of course, if he sunk the Belfast, he would be a hero when he got back to Germany.

Ridell told the lookouts to watch for torpedo tracks, then he told the hydrophone operator to monitor the sounds and bearings of the torpedoes. His assistants stood over a plotting table, pencils, protractors, slide rules in hand. The Navigator shouted, "35 minutes to safety sir." The microphone operator 's team had finished their calculations. He informed the Skipper. "Diverging angles sir. He's fired them in a fan pattern."

Ridell thought to himself, this Jerry knows what he's doing. The two outer torpedoes stopped him from turning the Belfast, the two inner ones would blow his stern apart. Now one of the loudspeakers crackled. It was the mast lookout.

"I can see the torpedo tracks. One either side of the ship about 50 yards out. But there's only one track astern, sir.

Quickly, the hydrophone operator jumped in. "He's right sir. One of the astern torpedoes has dropped out.

The Scottish yeoman on the other side of the bridge said to no one in particular, "I told you sassenachs," (in his strong Fife accent). "It's oor mental basking sharks, they'll eat anything."

Ridell glowered and smiled at the same time.

The same loudspeaker crackled again. "The torpedo track, Skipper. It's curving to starboard."

Ridell sprinted to the starboard bridge wing. He didn't need to use his binoculars to see the torpedo track curving fractionally. Now if he could just move the Belfast's bulk to port without throwing the stern to starboard. The best way would be engines.

"Quartermaster, Port engine, half ahead."

"Helmsman steer 269 degrees."

The helmsman thought. "Jesus Christ, that's the smallest course change I've ever heard. What good will that do?"

Before the bridge crew could shout their compliance, Ridell screamed again. "Port engine, full ahead, helmsman. Return to course 270. "He could see the torpedo track running parallel to his ship, but a few yards to starboard of it. His quick actions had moved the

10,000 tons of the Belfast several yards to the south. Now he prayed the torpedo was not fitted with the new-fangled proximity fuses. A loud thud and huge column of water told him his prayer was in vain.

Redemption

The bridge crew felt the deck move under their feet. The quartermaster knew the Skipper's first concern would be speed and engines. He quickly scanned the control panels. "No drop off in speed, steam at full pressure, engines at full revs." He shouted for everyone to hear. The captain grabbed the microphone for the public address systems. "All engine rooms, damage reports." All compartments reported no damage, bar one. There was no reply from the main engine room. That compartment was directly abreast of the torpedo explosion.

Ridell shouted into the microphone. "O'Hara, no reply from main engine room." While he waited on O'Hara's reply he beckoned the navigator. "How long to safety now?"

"30 minutes sir," he replied.

"God," thought Ridell. "Had all that happened in only 10 minutes, it felt like hours. "

Within a few minutes O'Hara arrived at the control platform above the engine room. From here the compartment's controls could be adjusted and a barrage of gauges could monitor the engineering systems. But, more importantly there were observation windows to see into the compartment. A few seconds after O'Hara, a leading seaman from the damage control department arrived. They checked the gauges and saw all systems were running at one hundred per cent. O'Hara quickly reported all systems okay to the bridge. Then the leading seaman shouted him over to the observation window. He could see the compartment had not escaped the explosion unscathed. There was dust and debris everywhere. There was steam, spray and broken lighting, but they could vaguely see the 5 operators lying unconscious or groggy on the lower decks. Alarmingly, they also saw seawater gushing in through a broken inlet pipe. Not enough to trip the engines out, but it would drown the men if they stayed on the lower deck. Then the damaged pipework burst apart. Double the amount of water was blasting in. Now the engines were in danger.

25 Minutes to Safety

O'Hara turned away from the viewing port and picked up the receiver to the bridge. He informed the Skipper of the situation, and the Skipper updated him about the perusing e-boats. "It's 25 minutes till we reach safety, Petty Officer. I'm ordering you not to open the hatches, O'Hara."

The petty officer replied, "I understand sir." O'Hara felt he was damned if he did, and damned if he didn't.

The leading seaman shouted to O'Hara "I thought you said there were 5 men in there. I see 6." O'Hara turned and looked through the window. Sure enough, there was a dark figure in there. Hard to see him through the mist and dust, but definitely someone. "Christ O'Hara, have you got a bloody highlander in there," said the leading seaman.

"What do you mean," said O'Hara.

"Look, he's not wearing a uniform, he's got a black cloak on, and he's got long red hair. How strong must he be. He's carrying the bodies up the ladder."

O'Hara was flabbergasted. The intruder was carrying all the unconscious men, one by one, to the upper decks. They were all safe from drowning now. He turned away from the window to contact the bridge. A few seconds later, the leading seaman got his attention again.

"Look," he said. "The burst pipe, it's slowed to a trickle." The mist and dust had settled now. They could see clearly into every part of the engine room. But now, there was no sixth person.

"What's going on," thought O'Hara. He decided he had to go up to the bridge and inform the Skipper personally. He told the leading seaman to remain there on standby.

The Final Sprint.

Ridell was out on the starboard bridge wing, watching dead astern. He didn't remove the binoculars from his eyes while O'Hara related the engine room events. He was pleased the ratings were safe, ecstatic that the leak had stopped, but was worried O'Hara had gone through a mental breakdown. "Am I hearing him right," he thought. "O'Hara thinks some sort of supernatural spectre has saved the ship" he told O'Hara to return to his control platform, while he refocused on the charging e-boats. They were hell bent on catching him.

The Skipper looked at the hills either side of the Forth. Both had concrete pillars, gun emplacements. The barrels looked like they were pointed straight at the Belfast, not it's pursuers. But of course, where the Belfast was now, is where the e-boats would be in a few minutes.

The hydrophone operator shouted, " 5 more splashes, sir, aimed straight at us."

Ridell operated the bridge optical range finder himself. The nearest vessel was only 3 miles away, but he was unarmed now. The rest were 6 miles away, a mile out of range of their torpedoes. It was their last desperate throw of the dice. The Scottish yeoman was standing next to him. "Well, jock, I hope your basking sharks are still hungry."

The yeoman looked at the range indicator next to Ridell's fingers. He saw the range, 10,000 yards. "Ach don't you worry sir, they will be."

The Navigator shouted out, "4 minutes to the safety zone, sir." Then he came out to the bridge wing. He addressed the Skipper quietly. "I don't understand sir, I thought the batteries would have opened fire by now. So they could get their range and angles of fire worked out."

The Skipper replied. "They don't want to scare off the e-boats. They want to lure them into the killing zone, and we are the bait."

The young lieutenant replied sarcastically. "Lucky us sir."

Ridell thought to himself. "Aye son, you're right. We are a lucky ship. Luck of the Irish. And we are an Irish ship."

"Torpedo noises fading, sir."

"They're dropping off, sir, " called the hydrophone operator, a few minutes later.

It was information that the Skipper was expecting. Meanwhile, the young navigator was frantically taking bearings on both bridge wings. He needed to be sure before he made his next announcement to the Skipper.

Safety

"We're in the protected zone, sir," shouted the navigator. "Both us and the e-boats." Only seconds later he saw smoke and flames erupt from the gun emplacements.

Milliseconds later Ridell heard their thunderous roar echo across the firth. He switched his attention to his pursuers. What a maelstrom he saw. Mountainous flumes of water were erupting all around them. Explosions seemed to be occurring every few seconds. Half the shells were missing their targets. But that meant half the shells were finding their targets. It was drastically more than enough. This was the first chance of the war for these gun batteries to go into action, and they were not going to stop till everything was annihilated.

The radar operator shouted that all blips had disappeared off his screen. Ridell felt emotions of melancholy. He thought about his German equivalent, and his crews struggling in the water. He had to push such thoughts aside for now. "Quartermaster, " he shouted. "Stop all engines." He picked up the microphone for the PA system. All hands, stand down from action stations. Those of you who wish to see a firework display may go on deck and look aft."

Suddenly watertight doors and hatches opened everywhere. Sailors were emerging from every one of them. Then cheers and screams of delight erupted everywhere. Ridell contemplated that this was their first victory too. But the Skipper had more to do. Into the microphone. "Petty Officer O'Hara, you have permission to take your damage control party into the main engine room." He wasn't worried about the engines; it was the five unconscious mechanics he was concerned for. Now to appease his conscience. "Bosun, launch your sea boats, pick up survivors, take medics."

The Following Morning. Rosyth Dockyard.

The captain was to attend a meeting with O'Hara at 0900 hours in the damaged main engine room. First however, he stopped at the Sick Bay. The Doctor confirmed the symptoms, concussion and shock, then scrapes and bruises from their falls. Then he had supportive words with the five young men, told them how their compartment had taken the brunt of the torpedo explosion. Then he told them a slight lie. How their quick reactions had saved the ship. Together they told him they couldn't remember any of this. He assured his boys memory loss was just one of the symptoms. It was time to leave. As he exited the compartment, he said to all, in a terrible fairy tale Irish accent, "the luck of the Irish to ye, all." En route to his meeting, he passed O'Hara's little bookkeeping office. On the door was one of Bernadette's posters. The Skipper patted her picture and said out loud in that terrible Irish accent, "bless ye lass, bless ye."

He walked across the observation platform and dropped down through a large hatch into the main engine room. There were sailors in boiler suits everywhere, repairing minor damage, cleaning up debris. Over against the hull was O'Hara, supervising a small team. As the Skipper approached them O'Hara said. "Pipework repaired, sir, valves replaced, and I've welded in strengtheners. It won't happen again. Now all we need to do is clear the blockage from the outboard pipes."

Ridell replied. "The two divers are on the quarter deck. I told them to wait for us." Five minutes later the two of them marched onto the quarter deck. Smoking sailors everywhere stood to attention. Brendan, knowing how informal his Skipper was, quickly shouted, "carry on." But they all knew to carry on skiving in front of the ship's captain was not a good idea. Most of them cleared off to find alternative hiding spots.

"Permission to go over the side sir," asked the leading seaman diver.

"Permission granted," replied Ridell. With that the two of them clambered over the railings and climbed down a rope ladder. Their back up team lowered down a basket full of every salvage tool Brendan could think of. Only 10 minutes later the pair surfaced. The lead diver removed his mask and shouted up " we found this in the inlet pipe, sir. " They passed the item up to the backup team. Ridell and O'Hara looked at the item, then at each other.

Captain Ridell ordered O'Hara to bring the item. Together they marched off through the maze of corridors and up ladders till they got to the Skipper's office, just below the bridge. As O'Hara walked in, the Skipper closed the door behind him. The two of them could now inspected the item in private. It was spread out on the cold hard deck. A lady's expensive black cloak. Hooded and with blood red lining.

"Look at this, sir," said the kneeling petty officer. He showed him the manufacturer's label. Embroidered capital letters, "B B".

"Bernadette Brandon" whispered the Skipper. Then he said. "But Brendan, we saw this being buried with her."

Brendan replied. "I know sir. I am not a religious man, but I believe everything happens for a reason. I believe Bernadette Brandon was chosen to look after this ship."

"Now, petty officer," said Ridell. "You and I need to write up a report on this incident."

"But sir," protested O'Hara. "When the Admiralty reads this, you and I will be locked up in a mental institution, for the rest of the war."

Ridell agreed. "That's why I am proposing that the completed report joins a number of other reports I have which do not get submitted to the Admiralty until the end of the war. Do you agree?

Brendan said. "Agreed sir."

The pair spent the rest of the morning writing the report, consulting diaries and inspecting messenger reports. No clerks were called. Ridell did all the typing. When the report was finished, together they placed it inside the Ships safe. They looked at each other, a mutual understanding had been reached.

Ridell said. "This file will not be touched again until the end of the war." They both knew the Belfast would survive the war. She had a guardian angel now.

It was time for the two mariners to return to their normal roles. Ridell had a luncheon appointment with the Admiral to discuss weapon installations and O'Hara had his engine rooms to inspect. O'Hara left the cabin, taking with him Bernadette's cloak and one of the Skipper's thick ink pens. First, he went to one of his workshops. He went to a deep secluded alcove. Reverently placed the cloak inside and welded a steel plate over it. Bernadette's cloak would never leave this ship. Now to get on with his inspections. As he passed each of her posters, he took out that thick, ink pen. Under Bernadette's image he wrote "THE BELFAST BELLE".

Harland and Wolf shipyard 1975

Maisie carefully closed the file. She was feeling very profound and sad. But her melancholy was quickly broken. From the hall outside came raucous laughter and loud footsteps. The technicians were back. They erupted into the room. Maisie decided to take a little risk. She said aloud. "Have any of you guys heard of HMS Belfast?"

"Heard of her?" one of the technicians exclaimed. "She's only the second most famous ship built by this yard. (The most famous ship's name was never mentioned in those days).

So, Maisie asked. "Do you have any paperwork on her?"

The team loaded her up with lots of non-classified documents.

"What's it for Maisie?" one of them asked.

"I think it is time." she replied, "that my son learned who his grandfather was."

The End

Epilogue.

Many of you naval bods may consider that the above report and happenings to be, "complete and utter made up rubbish." But of course, that was the reply given by the Admiralty, when journalists inquired about the report, upon its release, in 1995.

Was the Belfast protected? Well, unlike many vessels of her day she did survive the war. Indeed, she survived subsequent wars and engagements.

So many ships from those days are now lying at the bottom of the seas. The Belfast is alive and kicking, tied up at the Queens Walk in London, available for all to see. Indeed, if you look hard enough, and deep enough, you might just find one of Bernadette's posters.

Billeted

By Frank Chambers

"Mammy! There's a motor ootside the gate."

"Come away fae that windae will ye. It'll be the doctor for Sarah next door, she's due any day noo."

I did as ah wis telt. It wisnae a very interesting motor onyway. Mair like a van that delivers tae the shops, but withoot ony writin' on the side. Ah went back tae play wae ma doll's hoose, rearranging the furniture in the sitting room and putin' ma wee baby doll in her cot. "I don't think it can be the doctor," I said. "He disnae hae a bag."

"Nae bag! Whit's he daein'?"

"Ah don't know. Ye telt me to get away fae the windae."

"Never mind whit ah said. Hae another look."

Mammy wis busy wae her knittin' an didnae like tae stop in the middle of a row. Ah got up and went back tae the windae. "He's at Mrs Thompson's door."

"Whit did I tell ye? It's the doctor right enough."

"Naw ma. He hisnae gone in the hoose."

"Whit's he daein' then?"

"Just talkin'."

"It cannae be the rent man, he wis here yesterday. And he's no gone inside you say?"

"That's him comin' back doon the path mammy. He's got wan o thae board thingies. Ye know, like Mr Henderson in the Co-op, when he counts aw the tins on the shelves.

Mammy, Mammy he's comin' in oor gate!"

"He's whit!"

Only then did mammy put doon her needles. "It's important work for the boys in the trenches." she always says. "The least we wummin kin dae is make sure they hiv somethin' warm tae wear."

Faither says," there isnae ony trenches in this war, that wis the last yin."

"Wherever it is, it's bound tae be cold," mammy wid say back.

There was a loud rap at the door.

"Will ah get it?" I asked.

"Naw! Ah'll go masel."

Ah don't say onythin'. Ah know it's cos it might be news aboot ma brothers, bad news. Harry's in North Africa wae Montgomery, Jack's on the boats somewhere in the Atlantic. Despite her sore leg, mammy gets oot her chair.

There's another loud rap at the door and ah kin see mammy take in five or six breaths, wan efter the other, her false teeth chitterin'. Ah try tae help by sayin' she can lean oan ma shoulder. She lets me dae that sometimes when the pain is too much. Mammy says ah'm just the right height fur it, but no for too long as ah'm still only ten.

Mammy said "No this time hen. Jist you wait in the room." Mammy pulls the living room door shut behind her but Ah can still hear fine whit's goin' oan. Once ah turn the wireless doon that is.

There's another rap at the door, even louder this time.

"Ah'm comin', Ah'm comin'," mammy shouts. Ah could hear her dragging her leg across the linoleum and heard her groan when she put too much weight oan it. It wiz a while afore she reached the front door and opened it.

"Mrs Sutherland?"

"Aye. Whit is it?"

"My name's Jackson. From the council. Can you tell me how many people are living here Mrs Sutherland.

"Well, I've got three boys in the services, wan in the army, wan in the navy and wan daein his basic tr..."

Mr Jackson interrupted. "How many at this precise moment?"

"Jist the three of us, ma man, ma lassie and masel."

"And how old is your daughter?"

"She's ten. Whit's aw this aboot?"

"Clydebank was hit again last night, hit bad. It was worse than the night before, much worse."

"That's awfy. We could hear the planes flying ower when we were in the shelter, Ah knew it was gonnae be a bad yin. Is there many killed?"

"I don't know the full extent of the casualties yet, but there was a great deal of damage. A great deal indeed. That's why I'm here."

"Aye?"

"Street after street of tenements were hit. They were after the navy fuel depot, but it was the houses that took the brunt. I must inform you that I have been given the power to requisition some of your accommodation to house those who have lost their homes in the raid. You can read this."

Everything went quiet for a bit. Mammy must have been reading whatever the man had given her but mammy is no sae quick wae the reading, on account she didnae go sae often tae the school when she wis wee.

"Ah don't need yir paper. If someone needs a place to stay, we have an empty room, they can have that."

"I'm afraid Mrs Sutherland we will need two of your rooms to accommodate a family."

"A family, a whole family?"

"Afraid so."

"How many?"

"Three or four I should think. I'll come back later when I have more information. Good afternoon Mrs Sutherland."

I ran tae the windae, the biggest smile oan ma face. If that Mr Jackson wanted the two rooms it was aw right wae me. Since Harry wis away, mammy says I can have a room o ma ain. Well I didnae want a room o ma ain. Ah wanted tae stay in mammy and faither's room. Ah'm feart in Harry's room aw by masel but faither said ah wis a big girl and it wis only right that I should hae a room o ma ain if there wis wan available. Ah didnae like tae tell him ah wis feart, so I started tae sleep in Harry's room. Its been three months and Ah've hated every minute o' it.

When ah saw Mr Jackson getting back intae his van thing. I went back tae the doll's hoose and acted as though I'd been playing there aw the time. I pretended I didnae hear her when she came in.

"Oh my God, ah cannae credit it."

"Whit is it mammy?"

"Ye better run and get yir faither."

"Whit is it mammy?"

"Requisitioned it said. They're taken two o' the rooms. A whole family bombed out their ain hoose, billeted wae us. Three or four o them, he said. Pound tae a penny it'll be four, if no' five. You run an' get yir daddy hen. Run as fast as yir legs will take ye. He'll be in the yard at this time, ahin the toon hall. Ask wan o the men if ye cannae see him. Tell him he'll need to get hame right away. Tell him aboot the man coming and that the rooms hiv been requisitioned. Can you remember that word hen?"

"Requisitioned! Whit does it mean?"

"Ah don't rightly know, tae tell ye the truth. But yir faither will know. Noo aff ye get."

I ran as fast as ah could tae the end o' the street, but once ah wis oot o sight I slowed doon. I wisnae sure I wanted ma faither tae come back and say the family couldnae come an' stay. I could only think about goin' back tae ma wee bed in ma 'n da's room. Ah stopped runnin' an jist walked fast. Instead of crossing at the bank an goin' straight alang King Street to where the yard is, ah went the long way, alang the Main Street, half runnin' in case onybody saw me and told ma mammy ah wis dawdlin'. When ah reached the toon hall, ah passed it an' cut doon the wee lane at the side.

There wis four men staunin', just inside the gate o the Borough works yard. They wir smokin' n talkin'. There wis nae sign o' ma faither.

"Dae ye want somthin' hen?" said one o' the men.

"Ah'm lookin for Mr Sutherland."

"Tam. Is it Tam Sutherland yir efter?

"Aye. Ma mammy says he's tae come straight hame. A man came tae the hoose."

"A man you say?"

"In a motor!"

"In a motor!" The other men started tae laugh, Ah didnae see whit wis sae funny.

"Billy. Away and gee Tam a shout. Sounds like trouble at hame."

When ma faither came tae the gate he looked dead angry but Billy, the man that went tae get him, wis still laughin'.

"Whit's aw this about a man in a motor."

"Aye, tell us hen." It wis the man that sent for ma faither.

Faither gave him a right look. I thought he wis gonna hit him.

"He said we hiv tae gie two o' the rooms tae a family that got bombed last night."

"Yuv been requisitioned Tam."

"That's the word dad. I couldnae remember it. Requisitioned."

"Its happenin' aw ower the place Tam. Ah heard every hoose in the toon wae a spare room is tae take somebody in. We might aw need a room wursel if they go fur the Dalmarnock power station, and miss."

"Will ye shut up." I saw ma faither nod in ma direction.

"Sorry Tam."

"Will we get bombed daddy?"

"See whit you've started."

"Sorry Tam ah wisnae thinkin'." The man turned to me. "Never mind me hen. Your hoose is too far away fae the power station. Dinnae you fret yersel."

"Come oan." Faither grabbed me by the wrist and we set aff alang King Street.

"Is King Street too far away fae the power station."

"Aye. Way too far."

I was thinkin', the school is in King Street. Mebbe jist a wee bomb, at night when the place is empty.

Faither hardly said a word on the way back and ah didnae like tae annoy him when he wis thinkin'. We even took the short cut and crossed the burn at the steppin' stanes. Noo ah'm no supposed tae cross at the stanes, faither must hiv forgot. Even when he takes me tae watch the Glens play at Southcroft we always walk tae the bridge. "It's dangerous" he wid always say. "Yon stanes ur worn smooth, and slippery as ice."

When we got tae Toryglen Road we could see the trucks. Men fae the cooncil in overalls, a man in a bowler hat wae a bundle o' papers and army boys in their khaki uniforms. People wir comin' aff trucks carrying a suit case, others had nothin' at aw. The ones wae nothin' wir aw dirty, their claes manky wae white dust. Weans were greetin', some o the wummin an' aw.

Faither said. "We'll need tae hurry up hen." We started tae run. Ah could barely keep up. Ah wid hiv fell mair than once if faither didnae hae a hawd o' me.

As we turned the corner, we could see a truck ootside oor front gate. The army driver wis staunin' at his cab smokin' a cigarette, the man that had come tae the hoose earlier wis talking tae ma mammy. On top of the truck there wis three weans and a man. The three weans, who wir roon aboot ma age, wir still in their pyjamas and had a blanket covering their legs, the man didnae hiv a jacket, jist his shirt sleeves. They wir aw covered in the same white dust we had seen roon the corner.

"They want us tae take a whole family," ma mammy said when we reached the gate.

"Ah know it's a lot tae ask," the cooncil man said to faither. "Ye widnae believe the devastation in Clydebank. The place is in ruin. Street after street completely flattened. It's a miracle they are still alive." The cooncil man nodded at the truck. "They were sheltering under the boards in the close, thirty-two of them, most under fifteen. The next close took a direct hit. Three flairs came tumblin' doon on top o' them. They were at the back, under the stairs. The ones at the front are aw deid."

"And the close that got hit?"

"They didnae hae a chance."

Faither looked at the truck. "Aye, well they're mair than welcome in here. Onythin' we can dae tae help. There's two rooms they can hiv." Faither looked at me. "You don't mind comin' back in wae me and yer ma, dae ye?"

"Naw dad." Ah kept the smile aff ma face. Ah had a look at the truck. It wis three boys that wir sittin there."

"Tam!" Mammy wis trying to say somethin'.

"In a minute Sarah."

"How long dae ye think it will be fur, Mister...?"

"Jackson, George Jackson. Only until alternative accommodation can be arranged. Mr McNeil works in John Browns yard. Shipyard workers are priority. They're needed back the other side o' the Clyde as soon as possible."

"Tam!"

"Aye Sarah, in a minute."

"So the yard. It didnae get hit then?"

"It did, but mostly still intact. That's why Mr McNeil will be required tae get back as near tae John Browns as possible."

"Well that sounds aw right. Get them doon fae that truck and get them inside, they must be freezin', n hungry."

"Tam!"

"Whit is it Sarah? Kin ye no see ah'm talkin' tae Mr Jackson."

"There's another three o' them in the cabin."

"Whit?"

Five minutes later there wis seven strangers sittin' roon the good table in the living room. We were a chair short, so the youngest McNeil sat on his mammy's knee. Mrs NcNeil introduced everyone, sayin' their names and their ages. I forgot all the names, except Janet, the only girl. The ages were easy; nine, eight, seven, six and five.

Wae the rationing, we didnae hae enough food to go roon. Mammy set me tae work butter 'n breid in the kitchen while she went round the neighbours to see whit they could spare. Faither tried his best to talk to Mr McNeil but the man wisnae in the mood for talkin'.

The neighbours were aw sae generous. Mrs Collins sent some fresh made scones, Mrs Clark gave some o' her home-made bramble jam. Mr Donaldson dug up some of his tatties straight out o' the ground. There wis lots of other stuff that ah cannae remember but it wis the best tea ah ever had. It fair cheered everybody up.

Efter our tea mammy said ah should take all the weans to play in the field behind the hoose. We played bat and ball. None the McNeils had even played it before so ah had tae show them how. They liked the grass as there isnae any grass where they lived. We stayed oot till it got dark and mammy shouted us in.

While we were oot playing the man fae the council had brought some camp beds and mammy and Mrs NcNeil set them up.

Faither had taken Mr McNeil for a pint and when they came back faither had the Evening Citizen folded up and sticking out his jacket pocket. He slipped it to mammy as he came in and whispered to put it away.

Three months the McNeil's were wae us. Faither wis demented as the weans were always runnin' ower his vegetables, even though he explained to them aw aboot digging for victory. "They didnae know any better, havin' stayed up a close aw their lives," he wid say, but ah could see he wis disappointed. For mammy it was just as bad. She wis up tae high doh havin' tae share a range and a sink wae a wummin, cooking and washing for a family of seven.

Me, ah loved havin' the McNeils stayin' wae us. Me and Janet played peever and ropes on the pavement and we would push Mrs Thompson's new baby up and doon in its pram to get it to sleep. When the summer came I wanted tae go oot on ma bike. Faither said one of the men fae the yard would lend us a bike for Janet that his ain lassie wis too big fir. It turned oot that nane o' the McNeil weans could go a bike, but they soon learned.

The day the lorry came to take them away ah wis nearly in tears. Mammy said to Mrs McNeil that mebbe she could write and arrange to bring Janet for a visit. Mrs NcNeil said she would but nae letter ever appeared and they never did come for a visit. Ah asked if there hid been ony mair bombs in Clydebank and mebbe that's how they didnae write, but faither said there wis nae mair bombs and that it wis awfy hard to look efter five weans and Mrs McNeil probably jist didnae hae ony time.

Ah went back tae sleeping in Harry's room, but ah wisnae feart this time. I liked havin' the NcNeils stayin' and ah missed them when they left, but it was nice to have the hoose to oorselves again.

For links to novels and music by Frank Chambers see page 96

I Saw

By Jonny Aitken

I saw a bird of prey above me,
Circling the sun,
Talking to me through
the looking glass of number one,

Frost had thawed
bark had formed,
Went swimming out to sea,

What I saw between my eyes
was looking back at me.

Elegance and beauty
often rock the sentimental,
Born upon a programmed mind
the future instrumental,

Glowing heart I radiate
we fill our hearts with joy,
Diminishing the fear
Upon the rocks who sang the ploy.

Room 2B

By Hugh V McLachlan

Of course, I was much younger then, when I first met James Warren. Though broad in the shoulder, I was narrow in the mind. I had some growing still to do. I was, I thought, so mature, sophisticated and enlightened or – to use what was then the relevant self-congratulatory term – 'politically aware'. I – Alexander 'Sandy' Beecham - was none of those things.

In that long last summer before I became a student at Glasgow University, I had a temporary job at Lyons' Bakery in Govan, working in the section that made slab cakes. I cringe now when I recall the facile political statements that I was so keen to make and so unable to defend in the animated conversations which I had with my colleagues.

'There should be no discrimination of any sort. I believe in complete equality', I said. This provoked a lively response.

The consensus among my audience was that while, in general, people should be treated fairly and justly, that does that mean they should be treated equally. To discriminate is not, as such, wrong: it depends when, how and why we do so. As someone said: 'Disabled people should get bigger toilets than the rest of us if they need them'.

'What about sex?', a woman said.

'Yes, please', someone answered.

The woman persisted undaunted:

'What about your sex life, Sandy?' she said. 'Do you like men and women equally? Do think of them as inter-changeable in your wet dreams? Would you like to treat them the same in all respects in real life?'

When I was slow to respond, she said: 'You don't need to answer that question, it's your own business. But don't try to tell met that discrimination and unequal treatment are always wrong'.

'Don't forget about Kit', someone shouted out. 'Kit is available in Room 2B if you want to move on from wet dreams'.

There was a pause in the laughter and general merriment when someone said: 'A man who did not discriminate in his sex life between his own wife and his neighbours' wives would not be much of a husband or much of a neighbour'.

'He would not be much of a man', said another man.

I once said vehemently to my colleagues that, on average, black people and white people were of equal intelligence and that those who denied this were racists. What did I mean by 'average'? They asked me whether I meant 'arithmetic mean' or 'mode' or 'median' or '... perhaps some other scientific notion that mere manual workers could not comprehend'. I did not know what the hell I meant.

They asked me, in the case of the arithmetic mean, to how many decimal points did one need to believe in the equality in order not to be a racist? For instance, if one believed that the average intelligence of all white people was, say, 121.54 while the average intelligence of all black people was only 121.53 was one thereby a racist? Was it all a matter of degree? If so, what was the extent of the degree?

My tormentors continued: 'How does it come about that the average intelligence of different races always remains the same? What is the mechanism that produces and maintains this equality and maintains it over time?

A thought experiment was proposed. Suppose that at the present time, black and white people are, on average, absolutely equally intelligent. What if one of the sharpest of all the white intellectuals – for instance, they said, Sandy Beecham - were to die? The average intelligence of white people would, it was hypothesized, be significantly reduced. Unless, by some compensatory catastrophe, one of the sharpest of all black intellectuals were simultaneously to die, it was deduced that the average intelligence of black people would be greater than that of white people. How could I deny the possibility of such an outcome? Was it not mere dogmatism to do so?

I did not perform well in these mental jousts.

Someone asked me why I thought it was so important to insist upon a strict racial intellectual equality.

'Because', I answered, 'A suggested racist justification of the Atlantic slave trade was the supposed intellectual inferiority of the race of those who were the slaves.'

I could not counter the response I received. It was, 'As Robert Burns would have said nowadays: "A person is a person for all that".'

She elaborated. We are morally obliged to consider, respect and treat each and all other human being as persons in their own right, as individual moral agents rather than merely as members of particular groups, races, sexes, or categories of any other kind.

Slavery is, on various grounds, morally wrong whether or not the slaves are, on average, more or less intelligent than the slave holders and whether or not they are of a different race.

There is as much or more difference in intelligence within the members of different races as there is between them. It is not morally justifiable to enslave or otherwise mistreat those people of our own race, sex or whatever because they are less intelligent than the average person of our race or sex is. It would be no more morally justifiable to enslave or otherwise mistreat those people of a different race on the supposed grounds that they belonged to a race whose members were, on average, less intelligent than the members of our own race.

Once, when we were having a tea break, one of my workmates said:

'You're an educated man, Sandy. I am sure that you can read and write and spell. Now, suppose that I said: "A sextet of scintillating mezzo-sopranos exercised their vocal cords on the banks of the Mississippi". How would you spell' - and he paused here for dramatic effect - "vocal cords"?'.

I said: 'V-O-C-A-L'. Then I said: 'C-H-O-R-D-S'.

'Wrong', he said, while they all smiled. 'Wrong. It is: C-O-R-D-S. You're getting mixed up between musical chords and other sorts of cords like umbilical cords and vocal cords. Spell "umbilical cords".'

I got that right and they all laughed and cheered and applauded me. I laughed too.

On another occasion, I was queuing with a group of my fellow slab cake makers for our lunch-time meal in the canteen. I stood at the front of my group immediately behind two van drivers. One of them was called Joe Charlton, a large brute of a man. Joe and his colleague were talking about some particular young women in the factory. The content of their conversation was what I would then have called 'sexist' and would now call 'sexual'.

'She is clearly not a virgin,' said Joe, now turning towards me, ' Unlike Goldilocks here.' I had, as was fashionable then among younger people, very long hair.

I shouted 'Bastard' and moved aggressively towards him. This was a reflex action. I was shocked by what I regarded as the horrifying revelation of my shameful secret that, at nearly eighteen years of age, I was still a virgin. Almost immediately, it dawned on me that Joe was guessing or joking and that, if I had only kept my mouth shut, all would have been well.

In all my life before this stupid outburst, I had never before experienced any really severe physical pain. Was this happy state of affairs about to end?

Then- God bless each one of them! - my workmates, as if the move had been rehearsed to perfection, swiftly formed a huddle around me and hauled me back, away from Joe, towards the door. They hauled me away from him saying things like: 'Don't do it! … He's not worth it…. Take it easy...'. Any-one watching this might well have thought that only the intervention of my friends had prevented me from going for Joe Charlton's throat.

How grateful I was to be outside the canteen and not to be suffering physical pain.

Joe Charlton was a man who, reputedly, tended to bear very hard feelings but not, it turned out, against me. He told me that he really respected me! He elaborated his expression of respect by saying: 'You might look like something off the top of a Christmas tree, son, but you've got balls. You've got balls'.

'It's very nice of you to say so, Joe', I said. I meant it too.

News of the incident spread around the factory and reached James Warren, one of the factory managers, who I had recently met. Like me, he lived in Paisley. He sometimes gave me a lift in his car if he saw me standing at the bus stop. We became friends. It was through him that I met Victor Tonkin. James met Victor when he was a part-time mature student on the B.A. Social Sciences degree at Glasgow Caledonian University, where Victor taught.

James said to me: 'I hear that it took quite a number of people to restrain you when you tried to thump Joe Charlton'.

'That's an exaggeration', I said 'Or, to be more accurate, it is a total distortion'.

James Warren shook his head and told me not to be so modest. He said I should think about joining the SAS.

'Shush!', he said, 'Don't tell a soul, but I was almost in it myself. I applied to join, and they gave me an intelligence test. That was actually not too severe. However, there was then a test of physical fitness, strength and toughness and I must admit that that was hard: bloody hard. I passed, but only just'.

I was very impressed.

He said: 'So, it looked like I was in the SAS. But, at the final interview, they spotted a technicality! They noticed that I didn't have a driving license. "You need a driving license to join the SAS?", I asked. "Yes", they said "The Scottish Ambulance Service is very strict about that".'

My reputation, confidence and self-esteem were all boosted by the confrontation with Joe in the canteen. The thought that my workmates were prepared to make such an effort, at their own personal risk, to protect me makes me feel quite emotional even now, after all those years.

But I wince now too when I recall how I tried to inculcate my moral and political opinions in these people. How arrogant I was. How naïve I was. I thought then that morality was essentially subjective, all about 'values' and all about my 'values' at that. However, moral goodness and moral badness have nothing to do with our 'values', I have come to believe. If something is morally good, we ought to value it highly, but it is not morally good because we value it in a particular way. If something is morally good, it is morally good no matter how we feel about it.

I resolved to try to meet and introduce myself to Kit.

Room 2B was in the administration block, where James Warren worked. As a preliminary foray, I went over there during my lunchbreak. Several women worked in Room 2B. It was the location of the typing pool. I could see them through a glass panel on the door. Which one of them was Kit? I was pondering this question when James came along the corridor and saw me.

In very general terms, I told him the point of my interest in Room 2B and asked him for an indication of who Kit was. He said that no woman of that named worked in Room 2B or, as far as he knew, ever had done. I insisted that I had been told that she did.

'Did they say that she was available?' he said.

'Yes', I said. 'That's the word that was used'.

'I'm not surprised', said James. 'Let me show you something'.

He took me into the gents' toilet. I was confused. He pointed towards the row of cubicles. What the hell was going on? Was Kit inside one of them? It dawned on me, at that very instant, that 'Kit' is a name used by men as well as by women.

Then, I saw it. On the wall beside the row of cubicles, there was a notice. It said: 'First Aid Kit is available in Room 2B'.

For Links to other works by **Hugh V. McLachlan** see page 68.

Hugh.McLachlan1@ntlworld.com

Garnethill Girls, March 2002

By Henry Buchanan

A dull Friday night, last pint in the V—,
But no-one about, almost time to flee.
Then a tap on the back, *Lager, merci,*
Sit down with us, you can come along with me.

Intros, and fast talk, and carry-outs bought,
Her here's made a film, voyeuristic plot,
Nine minutes long, 'bout a girl's vacant thought,
Solemn music, with a great nipple shot.

Attic flat drinks, spliffs, and high high dancing.
Their Sartre-type friend larking and prancing,
His anti-war spiel this point advancing:
Géopolitiques, an oil and gas thing.

A song, and more drinks, a big pipe of grass;
A football huddle, to the roof en masse:
Clear, starry night, *Afghanistan ya bass.*
Steeples, sleepy spires, near sunrise, alas.

All on the floor to watch her in "Jholene,"

She glides through dungeons, smirking with a sheen,

Through fine black lace protrudes a nipple mean.

Come up again, next time you're on the scene.

Links:

https://brill.com/view/journals/djir/23/1/article-p105_011.xml

Margaret

By Anne Ferguson

Not one of the pedestrians, who occasionally passed along the quiet street, was aware of the elderly woman framed in the window of her top floor flat. It had always been a favourite place for her to sit in the early evening when the sun came streaming in but, now that she was too infirm to go out, it had become one of her few links to the outside world. She sat taking comfort in the warmth, gazing out at the familiar scene which had changed little since her birth almost eighty years ago. Nowadays, however, she knew very few of the residents. The people she had known were mostly gone and had been replaced by a constantly changing population of young couples and single people taking their first steps onto the property ladder. She was the last of her age group and now the time had come for her to move on.

Sighing, she manoeuvred her walking frame into position and slowly rose from a chair. Painfully, she made her way back to the boxes in the centre of the room. Beside them lay various possessions in neat piles.

"I'll have to get this finished, ready for David coming through from Fife tomorrow."

David was her nearest relative, the son of her only cousin Elizabeth who had died three years ago. The funeral had been one of the last occasions on which

134

Margaret had left her flat. Now David was coming to take her through to Fife and to the nursing home which was only a short drive from his bungalow.

" It means we'll see much more of you Aunt Margaret. Not just on high days and holidays."

She'd been happy to agree to the arrangements he had made for her. There was no longer anything to keep her in Glasgow. The few friends living in the city were now unable to visit her and were now only voices on the phone. In Fife she knew she would receive regular visits from David and Flora, his wife. There would also be occasional visits from their children who lived and worked in the area. And of course there would be the staff and the residents in the home.

"I'll probably be seeking refuge in my room," she thought.

There were some truth in this. Margaret enjoyed reading, listening to her classical L.P.s and tuning into her "wireless" for plays and concerts. These were pastimes best enjoyed in solitude.

She started to look through the various piles, selecting the items which were to accompany her. It helped that she had never been particularly sentimental and so she was able to pack quickly the items that David would dispose of once she had moved. Occasionally she lingered over the items which evoked strong memories of the past. The jewellery box which lay on the coffee table was carefully opened to reveal its contents. Most of the jewellery had belonged to her mother as Margaret seldom wore any. She recognised some of the pieces that she had received on her twenty-first birthday although some of the pieces were missing, having been given to a neighbour downstairs.

She had invited Yvonne to come up to select a couple of pieces as a token of her gratitude towards the young woman. Yvonne had been the one who had offered to get her shopping for her when she had started having difficulty carrying things.

"It's alright Yvonne," she'd maintained with her usual fierce independent streak. "I can manage. I just buy one or two items at a time."

"I'm going to the shops anyway."

"I don't want to cause you any trouble. You've got work to go to."

"I can pick stuff up on my way home. It's no trouble."

In the end a compromise had been reached. Yvonne would collect the heavier, bulkier shopping on a weekly basis while she picked up the odd item for herself as needed. The system worked well, and Margaret enjoyed Yvonne's weekly visits. They would sit chatting over morning coffee on Saturday mornings and Yvonne would tell her of her week's ploys, both business and social. Sometimes Yvonne would share a problem with her, letting off steam before stopping guiltily when she realised how trivial it seemed when compared to what Margaret was facing. The old lady didn't mind. It made her feel useful and she had always been a good listener. Later when she had eventually been allocated a home-help three days a week, she had listened patiently to the trials and tribulations caused by an inconsiderate husband and two moody teenagers.

"You're my therapy," Rosemary had told her on several occasions." I wish all my old ladies were like you. Never any moans and groans from you love."

Then she would carry on with the token cleaning programme. Margaret smiled at the recollection.

"Goodness! Look at the time."

The box was snapped shut and put in with the articles that would travel with her. Several other items quickly followed and before long there were only a few bits and pieces left to pack. One of them was the family photograph album and she decided to leave it to last.

"I'll look at this while I'm having my Ovaltine," she thought.

It was nearly an hour later before she was back, settled in the chair, her bedtime drink on the little side table and the album on her lap.

"I can't remember the last time I looked at this. Certainly not since Mother died."

She opened the well- worn cover to reveal the sepia prints of those long dead. A few pages later she saw the familiar faces of her parents in the formal poses of that era. In each photograph her father towered over the diminutive figure of her mother. She chuckled when she came to the first depiction of herself. Who would have thought that the fat little creature would have developed into the tall, skinny figure a few pages further on. In most of the photographs she appeared either alone or with her mother. Her father, who had normally been behind the camera, appeared in just a few fuzzy snaps. Occasionally her aunt and uncle would appear in the family group along with her daughter Elizabeth. Pages turned and years went by. Eventually she reached the pictures of herself in army uniform. One of them had been taken as she waved from the train that would take her to the camp. Another was one she had sent to her parents. It showed a laughing group of young women in uniform. She searched among the faces and finally found herself in the second row. She reflected on how much she had enjoyed those years. The camaraderie of the camp was not something she had ever experienced in civilian life.

Gradually the photographs became more sporadic and then stopped. This was about the time that her father had died. It had also been the end of her army career. She had returned to Glasgow to be with her mother. The next part of her life was to be spent in offices, most of it in a leather factory in the East End. Evening trips to the theatre and concerts had counteracted the tedium of her working days. Her mother had sometimes accompanied her on these outings but then she had developed heart problems and became too frail. At first Margaret had continued to go out alone but, as her mother's condition deteriorated, she had started to spend most of her evenings at home. Together they would listen to the radio, chat or simply sit in companionable silence. She felt no resentment. She had adored her mother and found her good company. Over the years her mother's health had continued to worsen and she was obliged to give up her work in order to care for her. Before long, nursing her mother became almost a twenty-four hour a day occupation. Her small group of friends had marvelled at her strength and patience, but she shrugged off their accolades.

"Mother is so easy to care for," she had assured them. She never complains and we do have some fun times."

It was after her mother's funeral that her problems had started. She had lost her appetite, couldn't face going out and had found herself crying at the least provocation. Her friends had tried to encourage her to start going out again, offering to accompany her to concerts, but to no avail. She couldn't even listen to her record collection, couldn't concentrate on her books and at one point had not even bothered getting dressed when she got up in the morning. She hadn't wanted her friends to visit and had stopped answering her phone.

Six months had passed before she had started to come to terms with her grief and to reassemble her life. Gradually she had started to enjoy going out again. There were visits to galleries, lunchtime concerts, theatre matinees and walks in the nearby parks. Unfortunately, this period of her life had been all too brief. Within a few months she began to experience the first symptoms of the degenerative disease which had gradually reduced the once tall, upright figure to that of the gaunt, stooped woman now seated in the chair. She had refused to give in, battling on to remain as independent for as long as possible. Now she'd had to admit defeat. Tonight, would be the last night she would spend in this house. For a moment there was a feeling of despondency.

"Margaret Scott. Stop this at once!" she reprimanded.

She placed the album in the same box as the jewellery and carefully eased herself out of the chair to begin the slow and painful process of getting ready for bed.

" But first I'll need to wash this," And she lifted her cup and shuffled towards the kitchen

Next morning David arrived punctually, as always, and found that Margaret was ready and waiting.

"I'll take this stuff down to the car and then come back up for you. Alright?"

"Fine."

A few minutes later and he reappeared with his son Tony.

"I thought it might take two of us," he explained.

"At least!" she replied with a wry smile.

They made their way slowly and painstakingly to the landing. Tony started to help Margaret down the first few steps while his father locked up the doors.

"Dad, I think it might be easier if I help Aunt Margaret on my own and she uses the handrail. You go on ahead with her zimmer."

Meanwhile, some of the neighbours, including Yvonne had realised that her departure was imminent and were looking out of their windows. They had already taken their farewells and Margaret had made it clear that she wanted no fuss. It was a long wait before they saw the little group reach the pavement. David opened the car door and then he and Tony went to help her in. The neighbours watched as some confusion broke out between the two men as to which side of Margaret each one was to position himself. The old lady was still smiling at the absurdity of the situation as they gently eased her frail form into the seat. Once her seat belt had been fastened, she focused her attention on the road ahead.

The two men got in, the car doors slammed shut, the engine started, and the car proceeded on its way to the corner of the street where it turned, leaving Margaret's home behind. Some of the neighbours waved. Yvonne wiped away a tear. Margaret did not look back.

S MAXWELL & SONS

By Palma McKeown

The workshop your father passed down to you
was once a music hall, haunted still
by the ghosts of old performers.

Among sacks of screws and racks of chisels
the strongman holds a church bench aloft
while a man in a loud suit perches

on it telling mother-in-law jokes. Hannah
the Human Candle winks at Mac the Minstrel
in doublet and hose, blows him a fiery kiss.

Oblivious, you plane a length of pine,
conjuring up a pile of shavings
with a sweet forest scent.

Your brother Sammy works nearby,
ciggie clamped to his lips while
his nicotine, shellac-stained hands

polish with the passion of a French kiss
and Monsieur Moreau's poodles prance by
performing astounding tricks. You lift a saw

and the magician gazes longingly,
his once-lovely assistant's legs
wander past, stumbling, tripping.

Now the building is gone,
Sammy is gone, you are gone.
But where are the ghosts?

Perhaps you wander with them
displaced by death and the bulldozer,
Sammy chatting up a chorus girl

in petticoats and pink stockings,
you yearning for a lathe, a brace,
the satisfaction of a perfect dovetail joint.

[First published in Prole, Poetry and Prose, Issue 31]

Twitter: @palma_mc

THE CARRY OUT

By Alex Meikle

'Shite! Shite Shite!' Dougie bellowed aloud without thinking, meeting the disapproving looks of two older ladies passing by. Pulling himself together, he stared at the merciless, blinking ATM screen. For the sixth time he read the despairing text:

'Balance £0.75. You can withdraw zero from Cashline today.'

'How can that be?' he asked himself yet again. A late, surprising, and very welcome cheque for £60 had arrived in the post from the Scottish Education Department, mid-week. The attached letter informed him he'd been underpaid for his yearly travel allowances which were part of his student grant. It was mid-July, and he was skint, with only his weekly dole money for students during summer to tide him over until the next grant in late September.

He'd hollered with delight when the cheque arrived and ran to the bank just round the corner from his home to deposit it. Cheques were supposed to take three days to clear, so he had every expectation the money would be in his account today, Saturday. It had been two weeks since he was last out, and he was desperate to go out tonight.

In anticipation, he'd phoned round friends earlier that day to meet up but, disappointingly, no-one could make it. They were either skint themselves, on holiday or had other arrangements. No problem, he thought. Flush with unexpected funds, he'd get the bus into town to the QM

Glasgow University Student Union. There would be somebody there he could catch up with. Failing that, he would head for the Griffin Bar in the city centre; there would always be somebody there he knew with the bonus he would likely hear of a party. The Griffin was renowned as a pre-party rendezvous.

Those plans were now scuppered and the pinging noise from the ATM attached to the bank alerted him to retrieve his card. Still reeling, Dougie Conroy walked back round the corner to his parents' neat, two storey council house in Tannochside, just outside Glasgow. He'd left there moments earlier a picture of optimism and returned deflated.

'What happened? Did you not get your money?' His mother asked, studying his face, when he entered the living room.

'It's still not in!' he replied despairingly. 'It's supposed to take three days to clear, and it was Wednesday I put it in.'

'Ah, but you can never rely on them at the weekend, it's working days that count, not weekends,' his father remarked. Both were watching *The Generation Game* on TV.

'We'd give you money if we could, son, but we've got nothing this weekend for you,' his mother said.

He was an only child and his parents doted on him, and if they could, they would give him anything they could spare. But it was mid-month and they'd just returned from their annual two-week break in Blackpool. Dougie knew full well there'd be nothing coming into the house until the end of the month; indeed, he expected his folks to be tapping him because of his unexpected windfall.

He went up to his bedroom, switched on his radio, lay on his bed, and listened to Radio 1. Another Saturday night stuck in. Life was crap, especially when you thought you were onto a promise. Listening to a prog rock band in concert, he drifted asleep.

His mother shook him awake. 'Listen, your father found three quid in one of his jackets. Will that be enough to get you out?'

He came alive instantly. 'Ah mom that's incredible! Yeah, that'll do, thanks.'

She smiled and left the room happy he was happy. It was emblematic of their love for him, that while he'd drowsed upstairs, both his parents had scoured coats, jackets, handbags, and the backs of chairs to get him some cash for a night out.

Three pounds wouldn't suffice for Glasgow, but it would get him four or five pints in what was his Plan B when he couldn't afford the big city, namely the steel town of Motherwell, a couple of miles up the road, where he'd went to school and knew quite a few people. He worked the house phone, calling three guys in succession who lived there, to see if they were available. The first didn't answer. He spoke to the mother of the second who informed Dougie he was away fishing for the weekend with his dad, while the third was just about to leave to go to the pictures with his girlfriend.

'Fuck! Is there nobody around?' he muttered in frustration after the last call. But he was only briefly put off. He knew he would meet someone, even if it was only a casual acquaintance.

*

The *Railway Tavern* was reasonably busy at just after eight on a Saturday night. It was mainly an old man's pub, but quite a few students and other younger people frequented it as well. Dougie's bad run continued, however, as he walked into the horseshoe shaped bar in the centre of town, because it was just the older guys drinking, chatting, or playing pool at a side table. The only women on the premises were two barmaids.

'It can only liven up and get better', he thought to himself as he ordered a pint of heavy.

It didn't, however, as time went by and only a succession of older men came and went. As he nursed his beer, every time the saloon doors opened, he turned hoping to see a familiar face or even an attractive woman, but it was only another bald or greying man. Dougie was learning the hard way that, unless you were a chronic alcoholic fixated only on liquor, drinking on your own in a busy bar could be a soul-destroying, very lonely experience.

Just before ten, Dougie resolved to give up and get the bus home; besides his folk's limited money was running out. He quaffed a generous quantity of his beer, nearly draining his glass, when he heard the doors open. Looking over, with not much optimism, his spirits lifted when he saw the large figure of Frank Mackenzie stride into the bar. "Big Frank" was over six feet, a full head taller than Dougie, with long flaxen hair that descended to his collar. He was the brother of the first guy he'd phoned without a response earlier. Seeing Him, and to Dougie's immense relief, Frank came over.

'How's it going, Dougie?'

'All right, yourself?'

'Fine, thanks.'

'I phoned your John earlier, but nobody was in.'

'Aye, him, my ma, Cathy and Betty are all away to the caravan in Troon this weekend. I'm just back from a mates.'

'Oh, ok, that explains' the no answer. Pint?'

'Aye, lager.'

He had enough to buy a round for the two of them, on the hopeful assumption that Frank would get him back, so he ordered two more pints.

Frank was 25, several years older than Dougie and was doing a post-graduate degree in philosophy at Strathclyde University. Dougie was about to enter third year at Glasgow University studying social sciences, so, Frank and he had a lot in common. Frank's younger brother, John, who Dougie had met in the *Tavern* and became friends with, enjoyed a smoke and would often invite Dougie back to his house for some "draw". It was during one of these post-pub sessions back in John's bedroom, with a continuous assembly line of joints being rolled, that he'd met Frank.

Now he had Frank as company, Dougie relaxed and, inevitably, the two of them started talking about their respective courses before moving onto politics. As both were quite left-wing, they agreed on the shortcomings of the governing Labour Party and the dangers of the Tories under Margaret Thatcher coming to power.

At half-past ten, to Dougie's great relief, Frank bought a return round. They went on to talk about music and at 10.45 the bell went for last orders. For the first five minutes after that neither man flinched but kept on discussing whether the Floyd's *Wish you were Here* was better than *Dark side of the Moon* until Dougie cracked first and said:

'Look, Frank, I'm pink lint. I got a late backdated travel allowance cheque this week, but it's not come through, yet. If you get us another pint, I'll make it up to you later in the week.'

Frank shook his head ruefully. 'Sorry, pal, I'm in the same boat, totally rooked. My next Giro's not till Tuesday. I'd only enough spare to get that last round.'

'Aw well,' Dougie responded, 'what would we expect in the middle of July eh? Every sod's rooked.'

They supped their pints in reflective silence until Frank said:

'Tell you what though, I know where John's hid his stash of draw. He's not going to take it to the caravan with the family. He's also got cans in the fridge. Do you want to come back?'

The prospect of dope and booze till the wee small hours, on this otherwise barren night, enthralled Dougie, but he did say cautiously:

'Will John not take a flaky if we smoke his draw and drink his booze?'

Frank laughed dismissively. 'Listen, the number of times that wee bastards' smoked my draw and tanked my booze when I'm not there,' he waved a hand in the air, 'must be at least six times! Besides, I'll replace the cans next week and we'll not smoke all his weed. Up for it?'

Reassured, Dougie nodded vigorously. Draining the last of his pint, he said: 'Let's go.'

*

It was twenty minutes' walk to Frank's mother's house (their father had passed away from heart failure years earlier) which was in the large council housing estate of North Motherwell. Passing through an endless succession of streets and avenues of uniform grey-green houses, they arrived at the long-curved avenue where Frank stayed in the middle of the sprawling estate.

Unlocking the front door and gesturing for Dougie to go into the living room, Frank said: 'I'll go upstairs and get the stash. Put the telly on if you want.'

For all the times, Dougie had been in this house, he'd never been in the front room; he'd always gone straight to John's room for a dope session. The living room was just like his mother's: neat, tidy, typical '70's style with matching furniture, walls painted beige and a large, rented TV in the corner. He knew it was rented as it had a prominent *Radio Rentals* sticker above the screen.

He switched on the telly and sat on a floral-patterned armchair. Golf was on BBC1, a sport he had no interest in. Getting up from the chair, he switched over to BBC2 which was showing some '50s black and white movie. ITV had a US cop show. That was it; three channels.

'There's fuck all on the box,' Dougie shouted up to Frank.

'I'll bring some sounds down,' the latter replied to the accompaniment of a flushing toilet.

Dougie went over to the radiogram with its enclosed record player. Below the record deck was, what he assumed to be Frank's mother's record collection, which was classic over '50s west of Scotland fare: Sinatra, Tony Bennett, Perry Como, Patsy Cline, Jim Reeves, and a host of other country music stars. It was virtually an exact replica of his parent's own collection.

Returning to the armchair, he could hear Frank rummaging upstairs and then clumping hurriedly down the stairs. He barged the living room door open, his face flushed.

'The wee shite's taken his draw with him. There's nowt in his room!'

'Could he have stashed it anywhere else?' Dougie asked.

'No,' Frank was adamant. 'My ma or the girls would find it. Fuck! Bastard's probably having a fly smoke by the caravans.'

'At least there's the cans,' Dougie reminded him.

'Aye, true.' Frank made towards the kitchen. Seconds later, there was another disconsolate cry: 'This is no real. The cunt's taken the cans as well!'

Frank returned to the room, dejected. 'Sorry Dougie, games a bogie, no draw, no booze.'

'I've got no money for a taxi,' Dougie said defensively lest Frank wanted him to leave; it was a good seven miles' walk to Tannochside.

'No problem, you can kip on top of John's bed. I'll get you a sleeping bag.'

They stayed up for a further hour listening to Hawkwind, Zeppelin and some Zappa. But bereft of the much-anticipated dope and booze, the conversation was desultory. Finally, Frank yawned. 'Listen man, I'm gonny get some zeds.'

'No problem, I'm knackered myself.'

'Sorry about tonight.'

'Don't worry about it, these things happen.'

*

150

Frank gave Dougie a rather tattered sleeping bag which he laid on top of John's bed. Undressing to his underpants, he looked around at the garish collection of sci-fi posters that adorned the walls and the array of albums around the room, many of which had provided the base for rolling joints, before putting the light out and lying on top of the sleeping bag (he'd thought better of getting into it as they were some suspicious looking stains on the inside). After a few minutes, he started drifting asleep.

He was abruptly brought fully awake by the sound of voices: male, harsh and coming from outside. He gingerly rose from the bed, walked over to the windows, and gently pulled back the corner of one curtain. Two guys, with unfashionably short-cropped hair, one wearing a leather jacket, the other a denim jacket, both smoking cigarettes, were standing in the middle of the road. They were shouting and gesturing up the road in front of them. Two plastic bags, which Dougie guessed contained cans of beer, were lying on the tarmac in front of them. All the houses on both sides of the avenue were in darkness.

He couldn't see who they were shouting at as the avenue curved just in front of them and he couldn't see any further from his angle at the window. The bedroom door opened, and Frank, obviously alerted to the commotion outside, came in, also dressed only in his underpants.

'What's going on?' He asked.

'Two guys out there in the middle of the street, shouting and bawling at somebody up the road. Looks like they've got a cargo with them.'

Frank stood behind him. The shouting from the two guys was getting louder. 'Come ahead ye a wanks!' The guy in the leather jacket yelled. They could hear only muffled response, but it prompted the two guys outside to run up the road and confront whoever their adversaries were, out of sight of Dougie and Frank.

'Look at that carry out man and we're dying of thirst here!' Frank muttered longingly. 'Ah fuck it.' He left the room. Dougie couldn't quite believe what he thought Frank was going to do. He could still hear muffled noises off, but otherwise the avenue was deserted.

He heard Frank descending the stairs, then half a minute later, the front door being stealthily opened. With his heart pounding, he watched Frank, barefooted, but now with his jeans on, walk up the garden path, make an agile bound across the waist high fence, pause, steal a quick glance up the avenue, move forward and very quickly pick up the two fully laden carrier bags, before, once again vaulting the fence, swiftly walk back up the path, and softly close the front door. It was over in seconds. He heard him coming back up the stairs and enter the room.

'Fuck sake man, they'll massacre us!' Dougie remonstrated with Frank as he placed the two bags beside the bed.

'If we keep stum we'll be ok, there's a dozen houses around; there not going to kick every door in.'

As Dougie resumed nervously keeping watch at the window, Frank rummaged through the bags. 'Crap,' he muttered, 'its' Skol! Still, it'll do. There's' a dozen cans here. That'll keep us going.'

'They're coming back,' Dougie said nervously, now crouching at the windowsill. Frank re-joined him. They could see the two coming back down the avenue with cigarettes in their mouths, pinched but happy faces, hands clapping, singing, obviously having seen off their opponents. Dougie could discern a distinct scar on the leather jacket's face. These guys were heavy, he thought. God knows what was going to happen next. He could feel and hear Frank's breath behind him. He couldn't believe how fearless and casual Frank was, in contrast to the fear that enveloped him. As the two guys approached where the carry out bags had been, Frank muttered: 'now the fun starts.'

Removing the cigarettes from their mouths, the two guys started looking around them. The guy in the denim jacket spoke first: 'It was here, wasn't it?'

'Aye,' the other responded, 'in the middle of the road.' He looked up. Dougie and Frank ducked below the sill. They could hear them looking around the street, beginning to argue among themselves.

'You didn't plank it in one of the gardens, did you?' Leather jacket asked.

'No!' Denim jacket replied strongly. 'They were right in front of us when we ran up the road.'

Exploiting a small gap between the curtains and window ledge, Dougie and Frank resumed their view as the two guys continued to pace up and down looking vainly for the vanished cargo, bewildered, befuddled, but also becoming increasingly angry. They started looking forlornly behind fences and hedgerows, including Franks' which caused both to duck down again. Finally, after a few minutes of this, leather jacket mouthed the obvious:

'Some fuckers' nicked the cargo!' Which prompted denim jacket to shout angrily: 'Aye and I bet it's one of these bastards,' pointing left and right of him at the houses. Dougie felt like he was having palpitations, but Frank still seemed calm beside him.

'Which one of you bastards stole our fucking booze?' Leather jacket shouted into the air. 'I'm fucking warning yous' I'm coming right ahead!' Denim jacket echoed his mate and the crescendo of their voices reverberated round the avenue.

Then suddenly, a light came on in the bedroom of the house directly opposite. Immediately, the two guys moved towards the house, shouting, while Frank remarked almost sagely: 'He who puts his light on first is in trouble'. 'Come on then,' the two guys shouted in the direction of the lighted window. 'Think your fucking wide?'

The hall light of the house came on and the front door opened, the two guys running towards it. A slightly built man of medium height, half-naked, stood in the doorway and shouted over to them:

'Listen you fucking bams! Listen. That's my wean crying. You've woke her, my wife and me up. Listen!' He commanded again. The two guys stopped, and their attention, as well as Dougie and Frank's, was drawn to the bedroom where the blinds were now open, revealing a young woman in a nightgown cradling a crying baby in her arms and looking furiously down at the two guys. After a moment's silence, leather jacket put his arms in front of him and said:

'Aw big man I'm really sorry. It's just somebody nicked our carry out.'

'Well, it wasn't me, the missus or the wean! We're just trying to get a sleep,' the man shouted.

The two guys were now calmed down and in full contrite mode. Denim jacket apologised:

'I know, sorry, did'nae mean to wake the wean or yourselves, sorry big fella.'

The front door opened at the next house along and a diminutive, older lady with a shock of white hair and in a nightdress, shouted over to then from her doorway:

'What the bloody hell's going on? Do you know what time it is?'

'That's auld Mrs McKracken,' Frank said, 'she's in her eighties. On yourself darling, give them hell.'

The two guys were now in full supplication mode. 'Folks, really sorry, misses, did'nae mean to wake you.' More lights came on in the surrounding houses with further neighbours appearing in doorways. Frank abruptly moved away from the window, saying: 'He who does not have his light on now will be a target of suspicion,' before leaving the room and switching the hall light on.

Dougie watched, stupefied, as Frank opened his front door once more, walked up the path, still half-naked, opened the gate and said casually:

'Hi, fella's what's happening?' By this time a whole guddle of neighbours had assembled. Leather jacket replied to Frank: 'Some bastard's nicked our carry out. We were getting hassle from some cu...' Leather jacket suddenly realized Mrs McKracken was beside him. '...sorry, from some guys up there and we just went up and chased them away. We came back and the carry out's gone.'

'Sure, you haven't planked it behind a fence?' Frank asked, all concerned and helpful.

'Naw, no way it was in front of us in the middle of the road,' Denim jacket replied.

'Some fucking chancer passing by has probably run off with it, sorry Mrs McKracken,' Frank deferred to her. 'Nobody around here would do a rotten thing like that.' Dougie was amazed at Frank's chutzpah in front of the guys.

'I know,' leather jacket agreed, 'you people are decent.' He turned to Mrs McKracken again. 'Sorry to wake you hen.'

Everyone's attention, including Dougie's, was suddenly taken up by a police patrol car cruising down the avenue, coming to a halt in front of Frank, the two guys, and the gathered neighbours. Two cops were in the car. Both got out, with one of them saying gruffly: 'What's with all the faces?'

'These two lads have had their drinks stolen,' Frank responded. The cop ignored him and spoke directly to them:

'Your big boys, did somebody come up and threaten you?'

155

Sheepishly, leather jacket replied: 'Naw, you see, we had a wee argument with some guys up the road there and we left the carry-out just here, and when we came back, it was gone.'

'So, you thought you'd noise up all these people, eh?' The cop was becoming more menacing with them.

'No, you see…' Leather jacket tried to reply but the cop cut him off.

'…We've had reports of a rammy up the road, but it's been a busy night, so we've just got here, otherwise it'd be likely you two would be having a long lie-in at Motherwell polis station. Now if I was you two, I'd put this down to bad luck and get away from here pronto and let these people get back to their beds. Am I making myself clear?'

'Sure, officer,' Leather jacket replied beginning to turn round, denim jacket following him.

'Safe home lads,' Frank shouted after them.

'Cheers mate,' they both turned round to him before continuing to walk away.

'Right, let's wrap this up and everybody get some sleep,' the cop commanded the gathering. The neighbours started going back to their houses with Mrs McKracken loudly commenting: 'This place is deteriorating, I'm telling you,' before closing her door.

Frank closed his gate, saying 'goodnight' to the cops who only gave him a slight, almost disapproving nod of their heads. Dougie heard the front door shut and Frank came up the stairs. Entering the bedroom, Dougie launched into:

'What a performance that was! You should get a fucking Oscar for…' Before Frank put two fingers to his lips and said, loudly: '…Shush! Keep quiet for at least ten minutes and keep the light off as well.'

Adrenaline was running through Dougie, so he found it hard to calm down. He was also astonished at how chilled Frank was. He went back to the window, lifted the curtain and watched the lights go off in the houses (the one with the child was the last to switch off), the cop car leave after a few minutes and an almost serene calm descend on the avenue.

Frank was sitting on the deep chair that his brother, John, used to roll his joints. After about five minutes, Dougie lay on top of the bed, beginning to feel relaxed after the madness of the last thirty minutes. The two of them lay there in deep silence for quite a while. Dougie was almost drifting back to sleep, when he heard Frank get up from the chair and rummage through the carry-out bags.

'Bloody Skol, cheapskate bastards could have done better than that! Here,' Frank threw him a can.

'Are you ready?' Frank asked in the darkness.

'Aye.'

There was a brisk tishkk noise as Frank opened a can. Dougie followed suit. Skol was a brand of lager which wasn't regarded highly, but for Frank and Dougie as they greedily devoured their cans, it tasted like nectar. Two thirds of the way through his first can, Frank raised it in the air, and pointing towards the avenue outside, said:

'Safe home, boys.' Dougie echoed him:

'Safe home boys.' Before the two of them dissolved in laughter.

The entire "cargo" of twelve cans was wiped out by dawn. For years afterwards, and throughout his twenties, Dougie kept a careful eye out for guys with short, cropped hair and leather or denim jackets.

He never drank another can of Skol lager again.

Follow at

www.facebook.com/BattlefieldWritersCollective

www.talesfromthebattlefield1.wordpress.com

Battlefield Collective (@Battlefield_Col) Twitter